LOCO and the WOLF

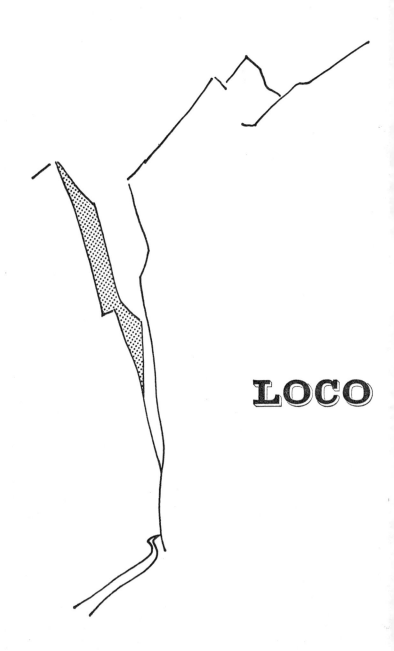

LOCO

and the WOLF

Todhunter Ballard

DOUBLEDAY & COMPANY, INC.
GARDEN CITY, NEW YORK
1973

All of the characters in this book are fictitious, and any resemblance to actual persons, living or dead, is purely coincidental.

ISBN: 0-385-05076-3
Library of Congress Catalog Card Number 73–79642
Copyright © 1973 by Todhunter Ballard
PRINTED IN THE UNITED STATES OF AMERICA
FIRST EDITION

LOCO and the WOLF

CHAPTER 1

Anyone accusing Loco Smith of being crazy drew an unoffended smile and a polite explanation that he had not been born that way. His branch of the Smiths, Loco maintained, were all naturally too smart for this world and his father had deliberately dropped him on his head early to insure that the boy would grow up on a more nearly equal footing with the boneheads he must live among in later life.

Wolf Garrison did not know whether he should get mad when he heard the story from the young man with the round, innocent, china-blue eyes at their inevitable first meeting. It was stacked in the cards that sooner or later Smith and Garrison would hook up. They were both gambling men and it was strange that their paths had not crossed before on the restless trails of the Southwest, yet it was fitting that when they did come together it was to share a cell at Yuma prison.

As soon as Garrison decided not to be insulted at the newcomer's suggestion that he might be stupid, an immediate community of interest sparked between them, with Wolf proposing that they present a united front against their four vulgar cellmates and the bloodthirsty population of the grim buildings on the cruel bluff above the confluence of the Gila and Colorado rivers.

Standing apart from the others, a sullen company of the most incorrigible criminals of the territory, Wolf Garrison spoke his contempt, waving a hand across the exercise yard.

"Look around here. Animals. Scum of creation. It's a degrading crime that decent men like us can be shut up in this bull pen with them. I know your reputation, Loco, and you never dealt a card from the bottom of the deck unless that was the only way to win and I'm sure you never fired a gun just for the pleasure of seeing blood run out of a man, but these . . . they swagger around bragging about the women they've raped and the children they've murdered. What happened to land you in here at all?"

Loco Smith sighed, surveying the high stone walls with distaste. "Man across the table liked aces so well he kept extras up his sleeve. When two of them in spades turned up in the same hand I called him. He tried to make out it was my fault and went for his gun. I had to shoot him, and that might have been all right except he had a sheriff's badge pinned on and the judge that tried me was his brother-in-law. Judge threw the book at me. Hell, I was only riding through Arizona to keep from standing trial on another deal in California. I must have been loco to get so close to this place."

"Me too, and I wish I hadn't. By the way, how come you put up with that tag *Loco?* Seems to me you'd resent it and being so handy with a gun would put a stop to it."

Smith considered the question at some length and decided that this new forming friendship demanded candor and thumbed his battered hat back on his yellow head.

"If you were me, Wolf, would you rather be called Loco or Clarence Chauncy?"

2

Wolf Garrison stepped back and his slitted black eyes widened in sympathy, his voice choked. "Cla . . . Chau . . . What would your old man call you a thing like that for? He hate you?"

"Some, I guess. He was an actor, my ma was his partner and it seems I spoiled her figure when I was born. She had to quit the stage."

"That don't make much sense," the wolf argued. "I've seen lots of fat actresses and some of them were good."

"Oh sure, but she wasn't that kind. Pa was a ventriloquist and he needed a cute trick to give the act some spice."

"Oh. I've heard about those but I never saw one. Could he really throw his voice and fool you into thinking it came from somewhere else?"

Loco Smith did not answer at once but let his eyes run over the exercise yard and the eight-foot-thick, eighteen-foot-high wall. Guard towers manned by riflemen topped the four corners of the wall that was unbroken around the prison except for the sally port on the west, the only entrance, closed by double barred iron gates. The cell blocks faced the yard, a row of cages each a tight eight by nine feet containing six bunks in two tiers, packing the prisoners in like sardines in a can. Rising over the squat building loomed the main guard tower, a tall frame structure with a sloping roof, open on all four sides like a bandstand, but the only music ever to issue from its height was the hard, chilling rattle of the Gatling gun mounted on the swivel base. While the corner towers were manned at all times by riflemen the Gatling position was used only in periods when violence erupted in the yard.

Loco Smith pointed up at the ugly muzzle with the revolving cartridge drum behind it and told Wolf Garrison, "Listen . . . it's talking to you."

Garrison looked at the tower and although no one was up there a voice called down.

"You there, Wolf Garrison, you stupid slob, why did you

3

get yourself caught? If you hadn't hung around to kiss that girl one last time you'd have been a hundred miles away before that posse organized itself."

Garrison's mouth dropped open, then he swung on Smith. "That you doing that? Keep on. I want to see how you . . ."

"Glad you can hear me, Wolf," the gun said. "It's lonesome up here and I get bored with nothing going on I can shoot at."

With difficulty Garrison kept his eyes on Loco Smith's mouth but saw no movement of the slightly parted lips, and though not a superstitious man he was deeply impressed with this illusion.

"You got to be doing it," he accused Smith, "but you're not making the words with your lips. How the hell can you make it sound so real that the gun talked?"

Loco spoke in his natural voice, not boastfully. "The old man started teaching me as soon as I could talk. You see, normally in talking the lips help shape the sounds but in ventriloquy the throat muscles do it. My pa said the words come from the belly. Watch my neck now." Again he pitched his voice to apparently issue from the gun and this time Garrison saw the Adam's apple and throat muscles barely twitching.

He whistled in admiration. "I'll be damned. How long it take you to learn?"

"Too long. Pa used to slap my mouth every time my lips moved a hair. Had it in his mind to use me in his act. Man, I've still got sore lips."

Wolf Garrison appreciated Smith's remembered pain. "It was my behind that caught it. My pap was a hell- and damnation-shouting preacher. It was a mortal sin to whistle on Sunday, let alone ever taking a drink or touching a card. Come to think of it he was an actor himself. Prayed all the time when he should have been out hoeing the garden. Kept Ma and us kids starved and dressed us from the poor box rather than getting his hands dirty doing something useful. I never had a new pair of britches until I was sixteen."

4

Loco exhibited a fraternal interest. "What happened then?"

"Ma died. That was enough for me. I whipped the old man and then took off with a wagon train heading West."

"Never go back?"

"Nor ever heard a word about any of them. Well, forget it. Al . . . that's the yard guard over across, said to show you the ropes. This end cell here is ours and you get the top bunk on the left."

Smith had not yet been inside the cell, and as they crossed the blistering grit of the yard he looked through the grilled door in dismay.

"Six stinking vultures live in that? Where's the pot?"

Garrison pointed to a tin bucket that reeked even at the distance. Loco Smith swallowed hard.

"Where's the water?"

Garrison flicked a hand back across the yard toward a wooden trough with a pitcher pump mounted above it. "Comes up from the river. Muddy. Thick as soup."

Smith let a sigh escape him and turned back to the cell. "What do you do for heat in the winter?"

"You don't. Summers it's a hundred and twenty in there and winters it's zero. Take your choice."

"This," said Loco Smith, "is no place for a white man."

"Or an Indian or a Mex or any other human animal."

In grave suspicion Smith ventured, "The food . . . how's that."

"Slumgullion mostly."

"I don't think I'm going to enjoy it here."

"Nope. The guards will see you don't. I just got time to show you the rest before the exercise hour is up."

Garrison led Smith away from the cell to that side of the yard where a hill rose like a cliff to form the fourth wall. Two wooden doors without windows were set in the face and Garrison stopped at a distance from them.

"That door on the left is for the Hellhole. They dug out a

cave behind, not tall enough to stand up in. Man crawls in and gets chained to a ring driven in the floor. The only air and light he gets come down a six-inch chimney they drilled from the top of the hill. Man sits in there waiting for a scorpion or a snake to drop down and bite him and goes crazy. A lot of them have.

"This other door is the T.B. hole. We get a lot of consumption here and the guards are all afraid of catching it. When a prisoner gets it they make another prisoner haul him in there and then bring him food until he dies."

Smith's voice held disbelief. "Don't any of them get well? Don't they get doctored?"

"Not in the year I've been here. . . . Now, over there at the far end are the blacksmith shop, the eating hall, what they call the entertainment hall, the warden's cottage and the guards' quarters. That's about the works."

"Thanks for the tour," Loco Smith said sourly. "It's not a place I want to spend ten years in or even ten seconds."

"You will." Defeat depressed Garrison's tone as this calling of Smith's attention to the inhumanities of the prison sharpened again for him the hopelessness that he had tried to blank away from his consciousness.

"Oh no. Not Clarence Chauncy Smith. I haven't yet seen a jail that could hold me."

"You have now. You just don't break out of Yuma. The only way out is to die."

Smith smiled at Garrison's bitter monotone and flicked a hand against Wolf's arm. "That's a mighty unprogressive attitude, man."

Garrison's mouth turned down further and he argued his negative case. "Well, say you did break out, how you going to get away? There's a hundred and fifty miles of desert with no water before you'd get any place."

"There are two rivers you could follow."

"Sure you could. And get picked up by the Mojave Apaches

6

before you made five miles. The territory uses the tribes as track-
ers, pays a hundred dollars for any escapee they fetch back."

Loco Smith was not convinced, insisting, "Somebody must
have escaped sometime, Wolf. There's no such thing as a hundred per cent anything."

Garrison looked at the blond man through narrowed eyes and
gradually a grudging, ironic grin dredged up to his twisted
mouth.

"I'll give you that. Yeah, one guy did. Sneaked away from a
night burial detail and hid in the reeds along the Colorado until
he saw the lights of a stern-wheeler heading up for Fort Mojave.
He stripped off his stripes and swam out to it and when they
hauled him aboard he told a hair-raising yarn about escaping
from an Indian attack. The captain was new on the river and
believed him, gave him clothes and took him to Ehrenburg and
turned him loose. The dope got drunk there and bragged how
he'd got away and the sheriff sent him back to Yuma. You'll
meet him at chow."

Loco grunted. "I don't want to meet anybody that dumb. A
burial detail, huh? How do you get on one of them? Are they
always at night?"

"No." Garrison lifted and dropped his shoulders. "Only when
a consumptive dies, they want him in the ground as fast as possible. Why?"

"If it worked once it could again. Get me outside these walls
even in daylight and I'll be long gone."

Garrison snorted. "You're as crazy as your name. There's an
armed guard goes with every detail. How you going to get away
from him in daylight? You'll get your head blown off."

Loco laughed silently in case the yard guard should hear and
be curious about such a sound within these walls.

"I don't know about you but I'd rather that than rot away
the best years of my life. But I'll think of some way to not get
shot. What do you say, are you with me or do you like it here?"

Garrison scrubbed his damp palms down the dirty prison

trousers and listened to temptation, sweating, then blew out a sharp breath.

"I must be as crazy as you because I'm beginning to believe you might pull it off."

"Good. So how do we get on a burial detail?"

Once committed, Wolf Garrison's long dormant inventiveness began to crowd his spirits up. "First thing," he said, "is, are you afraid of consumption?"

"I used to play poker with Doc Holliday and he was the worst cougher in the West. What's that got to do with us?"

"Like I said, the guards are all scared to death of it and so is everybody else in here. That's the way we get into position. Set ourselves up with the warden and the head guard by volunteering to take the food to the men in the T.B. hole and . . ."

"How many are there?"

"Three, the last time I heard. . . . We do that until one dies, then volunteer to sew him up in a canvas sack and to go on the grave digging to bury him. Once we're outside the wall it's up to you to figure what we do from there."

CHAPTER 2

Mitch Hamberg had killed three men in a stage holdup, had been caught, tried, and given a life sentence in Yuma prison. He had just paid for his crimes in full measure. After a year spent lying in the T.B. hole, after a month of receiving his daily ration from Loco Smith, Mitch Hamberg was dead.

While the first relay of prisoners ate morning chow in the mess hall Loco carried the breakfast basket to the isolation cell and was told of the demise by the other two inmates there. Mitch had gone free in the early hours before daylight. Loco left the basket, bolted the door after himself and went for the yard guard with the news.

The man was not Al, who for a guard had a more easygoing way, but Brodie, a sullen bulk of brutality who was suspected of deliberately introducing rattlers into the Hellhole for the pleasure of hearing the one in that solitary confinement scream.

At Loco's announcement that Hamberg had died Brodie backed off from him, afraid that Smith was himself contaminated, ordered him to the storage shed for canvas and sail-maker's needle and followed well behind with his shotgun at a loose ready. Then, with the materials, they detoured past the mess hall where Loco was commanded to call out one prisoner to help with the burial.

When Loco called out Wolf Garrison Brodie was not surprised. The two were dangerously chummy, the guard had noted, and that would have to be watched.

Garrison got up from the long bench and walked to the door while the others at the table watched him sidelong without missing a beat in the lift and lowering of their spoons.

Outside, Brodie called from a safe distance. "Give Smith a hand to sew up a stiff. March now."

Wolf Garrison met Loco's eyes in a brief glance and though neither changed expression the message passed. This was it, the opportunity they had waited on. Ahead of Brodie they went to the isolation cell, where Loco Smith opened the door, crawled inside and dragged Mitch Hamberg out by the feet and onto the canvas Garrison had spread. They rolled the body on its back and since it was already stiffening, Loco jumped on the bent knees to straighten them so a manageable bundle could be made. Then they drew the edges of the blanket together and while Garrison held them Loco sewed.

Brodie warned, "Sew the ends good so it don't slide out when you lift it. I'll get somebody to go with you."

He strode off toward the guards' quarters, keeping a wary eye on the mess hall where the men had piled out to watch, for entertainment of any kind was scarce at Yuma.

In these few minutes of privacy Wolf Garrison told Loco, "I hope to hell you know what you're doing. I can't see we got a ghost of a chance."

Continuing to hook the curved needle through the tough canvas, Loco said, "You just put your finger on it. Keep quiet and look alive from here on."

Brodie came back trailed by a reluctant Al and with the sack stoutly secured Garrison helped to hoist the unwieldy load onto Smith's shoulder, then Brodie returned to his yard duty, bawling at the audience to get back in the hall and Al took over the burial detail.

They stopped by the storage shed again for a pick and shovel, then veered to the entrance gate. There Al used a key on the big padlock and stepped away with a gesture toward Garrison to free the heavy chain and open the gate. They went through, Loco in the lead, Garrison behind and Al, stepping aside to where the wolf could not make a leap for his gun, waiting while Wolf locked the gate behind them.

The detail moved out, away from the looming wall, down the shelving hill toward the riverbank. In between was the unfenced cemetery, a barren stretch marked by the low mounds of graves old and newer. From the pitch of the slope Loco judged that near the lower end they would not be seen by the guards on the towers. The ground they crossed was a conglomerate of ancient river pebble, worn round by eons and cemented together in a mix that made digging in it brutal.

From ten feet behind Loco and Garrison, Al called, "That's far enough. You can put the hole there."

Loco Smith turned to look back. The roof of the near tower was visible, and while he could not see the head of the man standing there it was not his habit to take avoidable chances.

"Have a heart, Al," he protested. "A little farther down it looks softer and this sun's hot already."

Without waiting for permission he slogged on between the mounds, not that he minded stepping on them but the walking was easier over the more even plane. Al did not protest and Loco made another thirty feet and there decided not to push his luck too far. He lowered his burden rather gently, in gratitude to the man who had offered this chance, wiped his sweating forehead on his sleeve and gasped at Garrison.

"Your turn first. I'm winded."

Wolf Garrison obediently dropped the shovel and began hacking with the dull pick. It was a hard, slow chore to make any impression at all in the stuff underfoot. It could not honestly be called ground and it resisted with every pebble and compacted grain of sand. It took Garrison an hour to chop out a trench six inches deep, then Loco stepped in to shovel out the debris. The grave would not be deep but Al insisted it be at least eighteen inches and Loco reached for the pick.

Taking turns, it was noon before they reached that depth. The temperature was over a hundred and the sun relentless. Al had backed off to sit on a mound, his gun across his lap, his attention wandering, watching the turbulent roil of the muddy river and letting his eyes wander across it to the stockade of the fort on the far side. He could not see into the parade there but the distant notes of a bugle told him there was activity and he wondered idly if there would be a patrol riding out to break for him briefly the monotony of this desolate, motionless landscape. Nothing in sight moved except the two convicts at their boring labor. Then the pair changed places again and he brought his eyes back to them.

Loco stepped out of the shallow hole and the wolf took the shovel down to scrape out the chunks Smith had broken loose. Loco made sure Al was watching him, then, putting a hand against his side, arched as though to ease his back, at the same time throwing his voice to sound as if it came from behind the guard.

"Don't turn. Don't move. You on the ground, you're covered."

Al stiffened. Had he been on his feet he would have made a turning drop and sprayed the area with shotgun pellets, but caught as he was he knew he could not move fast enough. Loco's voice made sure he did not try.

"Don't chance it or you get lead in your spine. Just do as you're told. Throw that gun where you can't reach it, then throw your short gun after it."

The threat that someone armed was behind the guard was convincing. He saw Garrison in the hole, frozen, the pick raised above his head, gaping, first toward the apparent source of the voice, then at Loco, and again, quickly, over Al's shoulder. Without argument he tossed both guns aside and waited, his back tingling.

"Wolf," the voice continued, "pick up the hardware and move on. You don't belong here."

Garrison galvanized into action, dropped the pick and dived for the weapons, shoved the short gun into his belt and leveled the shotgun on the guard's belly, looking as worried as Al himself felt.

The voice said, "He's all yours now, boys, and I'll be leaving. Al, look around here."

The guard turned cautiously, coming around on his knees to face the intruder and saw no one. There was not enough growth on the slope to hide a jackrabbit and it lay empty, silent, a hot void. Al snapped his head from Garrison to Smith.

"Where is he? Who is it?"

The wolf lifted his shoulders and shook his head. "I never saw him. Didn't see a thing."

Loco Smith said explosively, "Ghost. Somebody buried in here. Must be."

The guard watched him narrowly, but the voice had been so close that he knew there was no possibility of a live speaker hiding so quickly.

"I don't like this." His own voice shook. "Let's get back inside."

Smith looked down at the canvas roll. "We got a body to bury. You finish the hole, Al, we're tired of digging." He crossed to take the short gun out of Garrison's belt and for the first time since his arrest felt that he was a whole man again.

They sat down together and the guard, under his own guns and the threat of the disembodied voice, cleared the remaining rubble out of the grave in double time.

"Good enough," Loco Smith told him. "Now roll the guy in and cover him up."

"Hold on," Garrison cut in. "We ought to knock Al in the head and put him down first. When the search starts if they dig up the grave they might only go as far as the canvas."

The guard swung from one to the other, gasping. "Me? Why? I've been decent to you all along."

Loco studied the problem. "You got another suggestion? We need a head start so we can't let you run back and raise an alarm."

Al edged away from the yawning trench, the guns following his movement, and pleaded his case. "Turn me loose and I won't go near the prison again. I'm sick of it anyhow. Being a guard in Yuma is worse than being in jail anywhere else. I swear . . ."

"Fat chance," the wolf told him. "I wouldn't trust you as far as I could throw you. What do you say, Loco?"

Smith looked from the guard to Garrison and shrugged. "He did treat us fair, Wolf. We'll take him with us."

"You are crazy."

"You said yourself once that I don't kill a man for the sport of it. Al, can you swim enough to get across the river?"

The guard breathed very carefully, chose his words with care, saying, "You mean the Colorado?"

"Hell," said Smith. "You don't swim the Gila, you crawl it in quicksand."

"Sure, I can make it easy." But there was an underlying doubt in the choked tone.

Garrison interrupted again. "So he swims across to the fort and routes out the army and where are we better off than if he goes back up the hill?"

"Get to burying, Al, if you're going with us." Loco watched the guard hurry at finishing the job and told Garrison, "He doesn't swim from down here. We take him downstream a few miles first. The current is so strong it will carry him another four or five before he can get across and it will be into tomorrow before he could find any place to report us."

"Well . . . I guess," Garrison gave in. "But let's get started. They'll miss us up there pretty soon."

"Brodie knows where we came and he knows it takes time to chisel down through this devil's playground. He won't expect us at dinner roll call and he's off shift in the afternoon. I don't think they'll wonder any until supper and we'll be well on the way into Mexico."

"If . . ." said Garrison. "You sound all-fired sure but we're not well on the way yet."

They tramped the mound down to discourage scavenging animals, Loco directed Al to bring along the pick and shovel to give a search party something to ponder, and the three climbed and slid down the sharper bank and into the reeds that screened the river edge. Fighting through the thick tule, gouged and cut by the saw-toothed lancelike leaves, they reached the water and turned along the shore.

They were hidden there from the bluff above until they reached the little desert town squatted on the bank and Loco assured the muttering Garrison in a low tone that they could pass unnoticed. He had deliberately timed the capture of the guard so that they would go by Yuma while the population was sleeping off its midday meal. They would have to get by the dock from which the ferry made its crossings to the California side, possibly float under it, but as they approached it even that obstacle in their path was removed. A flatbottom boat was hauled up on the shore, with oars for extra luck.

Loco Smith crowed softly. "Scot-free, Wolf, we've made it now."

"No we ain't," Garrison growled. "There's still the Apaches for miles along here. Let's lay low under the dock until dark and then try to coast down past them."

"Too much risk this close to the prison. I want to be clear away from here by then. Al, you drop those tools in the water now and strip. I want your clothes. We'll find some for Wolf farther along."

15

The guard protested that he would sunburn his seldom un-
clad skin but Loco was adamant, insisting that the man would
not be exposed that long, and while Garrison held the short gun
on him he shed boots, pants and shirt. Loco peeled off his
prison uniform, tossed it into the boat and put on Al's outfit,
then picked up the blunt nose of the boat and shoved it afloat.
On his order the naked man climbed into the stern seat, Wolf
Garrison took the center place to row and Loco sat in the bow
where he could watch the guard over Wolf's shoulder.

"Pull out to the middle," he directed. "If there's somebody
awake they can't see your stripes from there."

Garrison pulled for the middle of the current, aiming toward
the fort over half a mile across but drifting with the current. In
half an hour they were around the bend and out of sight of both
prison and fort and there they pulled in against a spit that
jutted from the shore. Loco caught the branch of a willow
bending over the water and told Al, "Out now and start swim-
ming. Don't double back. If you so much as turn your head I'll
blow it off."

"Don't worry," the man said. "I've had all I ever want to see
of either of you and I appreciate the chance."

He stood up and stepped out of the boat, waded and then
swam with strong strokes toward the far side. Smith and Garrison hung where they were in the mottled shade of the willows
and watched. Al's head and flashing arms grew smaller and
smaller and by the time they lost sight of him he had not yet
reached the middle of the river and was a mile downstream. By
the time he pulled himself out on the far bank he would be
seven or eight miles below the fort. He was barefoot and it was
doubtful he could walk far in the blazing afternoon sun. Loco
thought that if it were he, he would keep in the water, wade the
edge, but the time that would take would not bring him to the
fort before next morning. By that time he and Garrison should
be deep in Mexico.

"Let's go," he said, let go the willow and Wolf swung the boat off into the current again.

It was fast. Wolf needed the oars only to keep them from spinning in the whorls and eddies. Loco had moved to the stern and lay back, elbows on the gunnels, grinning.

"A good day's work, partner. All we need now is a smoke . . . Hey . . ." He sat up, probing through the guard's pockets and sure enough found a cloth sack of tobacco and papers. Rolling two cigarettes he put one between Garrison's lips and lit both. "I told you we'd make it, didn't I?"

The wolf grunted. "We haven't yet. We're not down the river and we're not across the desert."

"Easy as sliding down a greased pole." Loco waved a hand. "Nothing to do but steer this little boat and that don't take hard rowing."

Garrison, facing back up the river, straightened suddenly on the seat as though a ramrod had been shoved up his back. "Oh-oh. Look behind you now, genius."

Loco turned his head, then swung his body. From behind a bar heavy with reeds four canoes pulled into the stream, paddling toward the boat. There were three Indians to a canoe, two armed in each craft. Wolf groaned.

"Chato. I knew it."

"Who's Chato?"

"Means flat nose in English. He's called the best tracker in the country. I told you about the Apaches. Yuma, open up the gate, we're going home again."

CHAPTER 3

Loco Smith reached a hand behind him. "Pass me that scatter gun, Wolf, and we'll see how those boats ride with a hull full of holes."

Instead, Garrison kicked the shotgun farther under his seat toward the bow. "You'd never find out with a head full of lead. Those are rifles they've got. We've just run out of luck, and we can't hide. The worst mistake I ever made was to listen to you. Don't argue with them or you'll wind up spread-eagled over an ant hill with your eyelids cut off."

Smith continued to watch the canoes, approaching swiftly, sped by the strong thrust of wide paddles, and nodded.

"I never saw an Indian who could shoot a gun straight, but you're right on one score, we've got no place to go before they overhaul us. . . . Looks like he wants us to put in."

The stocky, square-faced Mojave in the center of the lead canoe waved a commanding gesture toward the shore and in resignation Wolf Garrison heaved on the oars and turned the boat toward the Arizona shore. They grounded on a mudbank short of the reeds and the canoes slid in to flank them, the bristle of rifles leveled and ready to fire. The Indians stepped into the shallow water and one man from each drew the craft back into the growth, out of sight. There was no need to tie them, the thick stalks held them in a tight embrace. The leader put one hand against his brown belly, then flung it aside, a signal that Loco should lift the short gun from his belt and throw it away. Loco chose to drop it to the floor, then lifted his hands and awaited the next order. It came as another gesture. Out. Walk.

Loco looked at the wall of reeds and discovered an almost imperceptible path through them leading inland. Half the Indians disappeared into it single file, then Loco, the wolf, with Chato and the others behind. The path wound up through a gully that would carry run-off when it rained, passed through the green belt and climbed a low desert knoll where a village of some permanence was established. Tule huts were loosely arranged around a bare yard scraped clean of the cactus that grew thickly beyond.

Indian men, women and dark-eyed children stopped what they had been doing to watch the arrival with lively interest and in the center of the yard Loco saw a thick pole driven into the ground, a figure tied against it. A small, wizened man with a dirty gray beard that hung low on his chest as his head sagged forward. He did not even raise the head when the babble of voices announced the coming party. There were no clothes on the skinny frame and his back was a burning red. He had been there some time. Loco and Garrison were marched before him and there Chato halted them, obviously to make an impression on them.

The Mojave spoke for the first time in passable English. "He from prison too? You know him?"

Garrison said in a strangled tone, "No he ain't. I never saw him before."

Loco spoke to the prisoner in a low, sympathetic voice. "How you making it, old-timer?"

The head came up then, slowly, painfully. The eyes were yellow, laced with bloodshot veins from looking into the sun and his quavering voice was parched. He read Garrison's stripes and the uniform Loco wore and cursed with surprising vigor.

"Lawman, are you? What you doing with these heathen fiends?"

It passed through Smith's mind that he might claim to be a prison guard, but the corner of his eye caught the black and white pattern of the clothes he had left in the boat, carried by an Indian as the captors made a half circle around them.

"Wrong guess, Pop," he said. "Name's Loco Smith . . . Wolf Garrison here."

The yellow eyes flicked as if the names registered and the cursing stopped. "I'm Gilbert Engle. How'd you know I'm called Pop? What you doing here?"

"Same as you, I think. How long have they had you?"

Chato interrupted. "Enough talk. Jailbirds go there."

They were herded across the compound toward a bed of glowing coals with a pot hanging over it, steam sending up a rich smell of chili and beans with perhaps a scent of dog. Loco felt the emptiness of his stomach and Wolf put words to it.

"We're starved, Chato. Nothing to eat since breakfast."

"You get back to prison, you eat."

The Apache beckoned the squaw who was stirring the pot and with a careless gesture turned the prisoners over to her for ministrations, then went to stand by the nearest hut, ten feet away from the fire, to watch. The woman came eagerly and her hands were fast, scurrying through the pockets of Loco's jacket, then through the trousers. She made pleased, cooing sounds and called to Chato in Apache at every prize she dredged out. The tobacco made a hit, but the money outscored that. Some of the Yuma prisoners had relatives who sent small sums to them and for a fee the guards would supply tobacco, whiskey, even an occasional woman, and Al had been carrying nearly a hundred dollars.

Chato held out a palm and the squaw took the money to him, chattering excitedly in Apache. Loco understood and spoke the language well and flushed under the names she called him, then made his face blank.

When both his and Garrison's pockets were emptied other women came to help with the stripping off of the clothes, joking among themselves at the thick mat of black hair covering most of the wolf's body, the pale golden fuzz that made patches on Loco's arms, chest and legs. Trying to ignore the indignity and ribaldry, Loco spoke over the women's heads as they unbuttoned and yanked.

"Why do you suppose he let us talk to Engle?"

"He was hoping the old man came from Yuma, was worth another hundred in prize money for him. Maybe we should have said yes. I don't think he's got much of a future now. At least we may get back with a whole skin."

"Do they take you back naked? What do they do with the stripes?"

"That's government property. They'll give it back once they're sure we haven't got a knife planted somewhere, or they don't get paid. But people they've brought back tell me they take their own sweet time letting you get dressed again. The squaws play games with you until you pass out and the fun's over. You have a trick way out of this, crazy man? What are you doing? . . ."

Loco had stood unresisting, letting his arms and legs be tugged one way and another, and now as the women retired to investigate the clothes, finger the seams for anything of value sewn in them, he stretched his arms full length, palms outward, down along his sides, tilted his head far back and worked his lips.

"Praying to the Great Spirit, of course." His voice was pitched for Garrison alone. "In a situation where you are beyond human aid, always call on the superhuman."

Chato watched him, as always bemused by the unpredictable white man. The way this one stood was recognizably prayerful, but all the whites he had seen in prayer were on their knees, heads bowed. Loco brought his head upright and put level blue eyes on the Apache, his lips parted in a half smile, and a voice from toward the rear of Chato's hut spoke solemnly.

"My son, you have taken an evil path. What you are doing here is wrong."

The words were impeccable Apache. Chato spun to see who spoke them. The desert beyond the huts was empty except for scattered cactus. Only a gray, tangled cholla, three feet tall, the bearded Old Man of the Desert was close enough, large enough to conceal the speaker. Chato snatched out his knife and stalked to the cactus, circled it in two leaps and stopped, knowing that he would have seen anyone crouching there. While the Mojave stared the voice rebuked him.

"Do not pull your knife on me. I will turn it hot in your hand to shrivel your fingers."

Chato dropped the blade, looked at the hand, then again at the cholla, and around at the Indians now watching. He raised his voice.

"Who said that?"

The cholla sounded sad. "You do not know me? You have called on me often enough. You have asked for much. Now I speak to you, will you deny me?"

For once Chato had a flash as to why white men prayed on their knees. His wanted to collapse. He stretched forward a beseeching hand.

"Great Spirit? . . . You are a cholla?"

"I am everything. The sun, the moon, the stars, the air. I am with you always. You cannot hide from my anger."

Chato sank to the ground, humbled and apprehensive and cried out. "What have I done? How did I offend you?"

"You have captured men whom I have sent on a mission.

Your greed for what the white faces at the prison will pay you have caused me the trouble of coming to correct your mistakes."

"But . . . But, Father . . . These people ran away from . . ."

A roar of rage came out of the cactus. "Dare you argue with me?"

The Indian shrank back, shaking his head hard.

The cholla's voice was heavy with the threat of doom. "The three whites you have here, feed them well, give them clothes, good buckskins, give them long guns and short guns to defend themselves and set them free to go on my mission. And from today forward leave their tribe alone for they, too, are my children. My son, do not cause me to come to you again."

The voice fell silent. Chato made promises; he asked for the favor of good hunting and good fortune, but the cholla would say nothing more.

Abruptly there was a frantic activity in the village as provisions were fetched, the emissaries feasted and feted, Chato's own canoe stocked for a journey and Indians jockeying for the chance to lightly touch these so unprecedentedly favored sons.

Gilbert Engle, cut loose from the stake, dressed, petted, pampered, hand fed by Chato himself until he could eat no more, found a moment when the white men were left alone while the flurry of preparation took the Indians away, turned bewildered eyes on Loco and half whispered.

"What the hell is going on?"

Loco frowned on him. "Is that all you have to say after the Great Spirit spoke out of that cholla and saved our lives and raised us up free men?"

"You must be drunk. That's the only spirits I ever knew that would have any effect on an Indian."

"You're sitting here, aren't you? Don't look a gift horse in the mouth. It might have better teeth than you think."

Engle chuckled, a ragged sound from a throat still rough from thirst, and chafed at his bony wrists where the circulation was not yet wholly restored. That was one of the things they would learn about him as they got to know him better. No matter how tough the going turned, the wiry old man would find something to amuse him.

With yet an hour's daylight ahead of them they were escorted back along the path and ceremoniously set off in the canoe, past the entire village that lined the shallow shore. Wolf Garrison paddled bow, Loco took the stern and Engle sat on the goods piled between. Loco, a tightness lingering along his spine, only breathed fully when a bend put Chato's village well behind and out of sight, then he sighed and asked Engle, "What were you doing with them? How did they get their hands on you?"

The old man lay back, his head resting on the thwart, and spat over the side. "I fell overboard."

"Overboard from what?"

"The boat. I came all the way from San Francisco to the mouth of the river, no trouble at all, then I switched to the *River Queen,* the stern-wheeler that takes supplies up for the army at Ehrenburg."

"You in the army?"

"Me a bluebelly?" Engle spat again. "Not likely, I'm from Tennessee."

"And you fell off the *Queen?* How did that happen?"

"Well, I didn't exactly fall. I was pushed. Minding my own business up on the Texas, admiring the moonlight on the water and them two brush jumpers grabbed me and tossed me over the side."

"They give any reason? You give them trouble in a card game?"

"No . . . no . . . we'd been getting along just fine. I thought."

"Did they rob you?"

"Yeah, that's it. They robbed me."

It was said too quickly. There was an evasion there. Wolf Garrison turned his head to look back at the man, then at Loco. Loco was watching Engle with more interest than he had previously had.

24

"You know, Garrison," he said softly, "I don't believe this old coot quite trusts us, even after we rescued him."

"Sounds that way. What do we do about it?" Whatever Loco Smith should direct from here on, Wolf Garrison would go along with, his skepticism, his lack of faith in his friend exorcised for good by the display in Chato's camp.

"If he doesn't level with us he could be a danger to us. He must have swum ashore from the boat, so if we put him over here he ought to be all right and we'll be shut of him." Loco laid his paddle aside, put his hands on the gunwales and moved one knee forward.

Pop Engle shoved up, reached behind and clamped his thin hands tightly around the thwart, saying hurriedly, "Now wait a minute, fellows, maybe we can make a deal. . . ."

Loco Smith stopped, righted the canoe as Engle's sudden jerking nearly tipped it over, and raised his brows. As a gambler he would always listen to a deal before he turned it down.

"What do you have in mind, Pop?"

The old man chewed at his lip, his eyes worried, then he took a deep breath and made the plunge.

"I guess I owe you at that, whatever it was made those red varmints change their ways, and maybe I can make it up to you if you want to take the chance. I oughtn't to, but I'll have to trust you with Jerry's secret. . . ."

"Jerry? Who's he?"

"He's a she. My goddaughter."

Fumbling through the pockets of his new buckskin jacket, to which everything that had been taken from him had been restored, Engle brought out a tintype and handed it to Loco. The bath in the river had not improved it and the photographer whose name and Holladay Street, Denver address were stamped on the back had not made the best of jobs, but the dim face looking out at him was a remarkably handsome young woman. Loco returned it to Engle.

"Pass it up to Wolf, Pop, and tell us how you come to have a relative who looks like that."

Wolf Garrison whistled softly at the picture. Engle explained, "Why, her daddy was a side-kick of mine from way back. Up until he died we were always in business together, started out freighting, then it worked into stage coaches and express cars and the like."

Garrison snorted. "Holding them up, you mean?"

The old man clawed at his long beard. "That wasn't the way we looked at it. You see, the big firms were always doing the little man, using the roads and running out competition. We, Dilly and me, started out to build a freight and stage line. He saved our money and we bought a used mud wagon and four horses, and we were doing all right until along came Wells Fargo. We were charging twenty dollars to haul passengers to Georgetown from Denver. That outfit cut the rate to ten and put us out of business." He finished in shrill bitterness. "What were we supposed to do? Lie down and play dead? Not likely. We swore we'd make them keep us in funds, and we did."

He was silent so long, fuming over the injustice, that Loco prompted him.

"So?"

Engle blew heavily, blowing the memory away. "So I spent mine. Never could keep two nickels to knock together, but Dilly, Dilly was a saving man, downright tight. You know how a chipmunk is about nuts . . . Dilly was that way about dollars. He managed to get together more than a hundred thousand. Then he got run out of Denver and took off for Arizona Territory. We were going to bust up the partnership until things cooled down some. He was heading for Tombstone, but in a little place called Phoenix he took sick. He wrote to Jerry that he was dying but that he'd buried his money in the Superstitions. Sent her a map and told her to give it to me."

Wolf Garrison sent a sharp glance back at Loco. "You got the map on you?"

26

"Did have, until like a damn fool I talked to those two men I met on the steamer. They seemed all right and I knew I needed help. The Superstition Mountains are rough and the Indians are bad there and these two talked as if they knew their way around the area. I told them about the map and offered them a third of money if they'd help me bring it out."

"And they jumped you on the Texas, took the map and pushed you over." Loco Smith sounded disgusted. "Where's your goddaughter now?"

"Supposed to meet me in Phoenix. I was in San Francisco when I got her letter and the map, so I caught the steamer and she's coming overland by coach."

"How long ago was that tintype taken?"

"Right after she heard from Dilly. I hadn't seen her since she was a little kid and she wrote that she wanted me to recognize her without trouble."

"Wolf," Loco called to the bow, "what do you say we head back up to Phoenix and help get the lady's map back for her?"

Wolf Garrison plunged his paddle into the current and veered the prow toward the shore as the last sun turned it gold and brilliant.

"Why not? We haven't a thing better to do."

Engle cautioned, "They'll send you back to Yuma if they catch you up there."

Wolf called without looking back. "You ever been in Arizona?"

"Only as far as that Indian camp."

Loco said lightly, "There's not much law there outside of Tucson, Tombstone and maybe Prescott. People are too busy dodging Indians to worry about a couple of men who aren't making any trouble for them. Especially if we don't advertise who we are."

CHAPTER 4

Geraldine Dillman had grown up looking after herself without the help of a father. When she was five her mother had thrown her husband out of the house and thenceforward supported herself and her daughter from a tiny restaurant on Larimer Street. After her death a year before, Jerry had continued to run the place but without much success. Her mother had been an excellent cook but Jerry found that she was not. When her father's map arrived like a gift from heaven she had not hesitated to sell out and board the stage for Arizona with high hope and confidence.

Nothing in her experience had prepared her for the shock of the bleak mud village she found squatting like a sorry ant hill far out on the desolate desert. To be sure, it was located near where the Verde ran into the Salt, so the community had water, but not a tree, no verdure, none of the green magnificence of Colorado. Where Denver's Rockies rose in white topped majesty, the Superstitions hulked to the east of Phoenix stark and unfriendly to man.

Tucson, Jerry had heard, was old, established, gracious. Prescott was a busy mining camp. Phoenix was nothing, its only reason for being, the confluence of the two rivers. North of it Camp Verde and Fort Whipple watched the Indians. To the east was Fort Apache and to the south Tucson. Phoenix was located in the center of the land the Apaches had always considered their own, yet oddly it had escaped the attacks that had struck so many isolated ranches. A fluctuating citizenry of at best two hundred continuously came and went on quiet, mysterious errands.

The stage had pulled to a halt before a single-story, adobe hotel, its roof supported by long timbers that had been freighted down from the mountains, protruding two feet through the walls to make the chunky building appear lower than it was. The driver unceremoniously deposited the bell topped trunk on the wooden walk, climbed back aboard and whipped up his team for the run on to Tucson.

Jerry Dillman stood in the red dust watching the coach depart and a hollow helplessness engulfed her. She had expected her godfather to meet her but the only people in sight were a few Mexican and Indian women in gaudy dresses and a group of loafers hunkered in the shade of the gallery that ran around the hotel. No one made any move to help her. The sun seemed to press her down into the ground, she had not the strength to move the trunk herself but because it held everything she owned she dared not leave it alone.

A voice behind her said, "Can I help?"

She started and turned, a tall girl, usually self-possessed but at the moment finding that Phoenix was too much for her. Then she recognized him. He had been on the stage. She had seen him in the eating stops but he had ridden on the high seat beside the driver. She did not know whether he had come all the way from Denver or had joined the coach at an intermediate stop and she did not care. It was a vast relief to see any familiar face and she gave him an embarrassed smile.

"Indeed yes, if you could find someone to take my trunk into the hotel."

He had a blanket roll over his wide shoulder and carried a small collapsible valise. He handed her the valise, which was surprisingly light, and hefted the heavy trunk to his free shoulder. The loafers glanced at him briefly but their bird-eyed attention was on the girl, taking in the long shawl silk dress, the tricky little hat with the wisp of veil above the red-gold hair.

Jerry held her head high and ignored them. She had been around the restaurant all of her life and since her fifteenth year conscious of the interest she roused in men and understood its meaning, and obviously in this remote place they seldom saw a city girl, comely or not.

They came into the lobby, a dark, narrow hall between the saloon that filled the corner half of the building and the dining room opposite. When her eyes accustomed to the gloom Jerry saw a woman behind a high counter, her face weather worn to leather, her expression hard, her voice stony, saying, "Sorry, we got no room."

The man spoke with quiet conviction. "You have room."

The woman looked his way. His eyes were level, quiet, his mouth a straight, firm line. She dropped her eyes to his hips, the crossed belts, the two guns swinging low in worn holsters.

"Maybe I made a mistake."

"You did."

She glared, challenging, her eyes the color of burnished mahogany, then she backed down and shoved forward an ink-spattered journal, indicated a snub-nosed pen. The blond girl wrote Geraldine Dillman, Denver, Colorado Territory, in a strong, bold hand. The woman turned the register quickly to read, still bristling, and when she looked up her manner had changed.

"You Dilly Dillman's girl?"

30

Surprised by the abrupt turnabout, Jerry nodded.

"Well now." The woman gave her a swift new scrutiny. "I took you for one of them floozies drifting down from Holladay Street. Why in hell didn't you tell me?"

Jerry took her revenge. "Why in hell didn't you ask me?"

The woman laughed, a loud, male sound. "We're going to get along, dearie. I'm Mame Carter, own this place and run it good. No foolishness in here." She turned back to the man still carrying the trunk. "And who are you?"

"The name is Lambert. Craig Lambert."

Suspicion returned to Mame Carter's face. "You two together?"

Lambert's mouth quirked. "If you mean, did we ride here on the same stage, yes. If you're asking whether we were acquainted before getting on that stage, no."

"I know about her . . . what's your business in Phoenix?"

Again his lips twitched. "I might be a lawyer looking for a place to hang my shingle, or a doctor come out to heal the sick, or an undertaker here to bury the dead. . . ."

Her eyes crinkled nearly closed. "If you was to ask me I'd say you're more likely the one who makes business for the undertaker than the man who plants the stiff in the box. . . . You a gambler?"

"Sometimes."

"You'd better move on to Tucson, better yet Tombstone. You won't make tobacco money in these parts."

"Maybe later. What room does Miss Dillman's trunk go in?"

"Number ten."

Lambert turned and moved down the hall, light on his feet even under the heavy weight. Before Jerry could follow Mame Carter put out a restraining hand and lowered her voice.

"You watch out for him, dearie. I know the kind. I didn't always have the complexion of an armadillo and I've had a heap of men after me."

"I'm sure you have. . . ." Jerry looked after Craig Lambert, but with this woman so talkative now she might be willing to give information that Jerry wanted. "Tell me how my father came to die."

"He was shot." There was no emphasis on the words.

Jerry was jolted but not truly surprised. "He didn't tell me in his letter."

"I know. Dilly didn't want to fret you over what couldn't be helped. A fellow named Carney heard your father had some money hid out in the hills and was trying to make him tell where. He pulled a gun. Dilly jumped for it and it went off. Carney claimed it was self-defense, but he took off running for the Superstitions."

"To look for the money, I suppose."

"I'd say so, but there's lots of territory up there. He ain't the only one trying to find it. Week ago a pair showed up asking questions about Dilly. I didn't like their looks and they said they had a map to where some money was stashed. They couldn't read the map right so they hired No Shoes Johnson to guide them." The woman's face wrinkled in a full grin. "Thing is, No Shoes don't know much more about the mountains than these birds. They'll all be lucky to get out of the Superstitions alive. . . . Did you get Dilly's map to Pop Engle?"

Caution sparked by this talk kept Jerry from answering and the hotel woman snorted.

"Don't be afraid of me, dearie, I helped your daddy write that letter. He was so weak he couldn't hold a pen."

Feeling more alone, even abandoned, Jerry said slowly, "I sent it to him. I told him to meet me here. It looks like he didn't come."

"Damn, I knew it. Dilly was sure he could trust Pop, and I said he's a man, ain't he. I should have kept it here like I wanted, but Dilly made me promise to send it to you just before he died. You want some advice, dearie? Go on back to Denver and forget that map. You'll never see it again, or the money either."

A sickness filled Jerry Dillman. To come this close and then have her inheritance snatched away, to have risked everything she had and be stranded in this hopeless place crushed in on her, was made more dreadful by the appalling heat. She said faintly,

"Thank you. I'll have to think. I'll go wash up now, then I'd like to visit the cemetery."

Mame Carter looked equally stricken. "You won't find anything fancy. I put up a board over Dilly's grave but we don't have no stone carvers."

"It's all right." The girl's voice choked, but not for her father's sorry end. She did not deceive herself, she did not remember even what he had looked like. Still, she would go and pay her respect because he had been the last relative she had.

Craig Lambert came back, lifted his hat and under the guise of courtesy gave her a quick, probing scrutiny, then left the hotel. Jerry found the room, removed her dress and washed with the tepid water from the pitcher, sat on the sagging bed and brushed out her hair. That was always a pleasure, the tingle at her scalp, the comfort of pulling the brush through the long, thick strands. Gradually she quieted the churning inside her, finally sighed, lifted her chin, bound up her hair and dressed and left the room.

The lobby was empty now. She sneaked a look at the register and with a strange relief saw that Lambert had signed it, then went on to the shaded gallery. The loafers made speculative comments too low for her to hear and she stepped down into the deep dust rather than use the boardwalk so close to them and turned up the wide track toward the far end of the scraggly town.

The buildings she passed were single-story 'dobe, some boasting false fronts above the wooden awning. Three freight wagons moving sluggishly stirred dust powder into the hot, windless air and she returned to the slatted walk, reached the end of it without seeing anyone on foot, and continued along the open roadway to the little knoll with a rough, rock, foot-high wall around it to distinguish the graveyard from the desert.

Inside, the ground was a hard-baked crust of little-used paths and perhaps twenty low mounds, a high percentage for so young and tiny a town, the headboards in various stages of bleaching. She found her father's grave at the end of the last row, the board a little newer, the lettering burned into it not yet weathered by the flying grit.

Daniel David Dillman
Came from heaven, went to hell
Some will say was just as well

She had not known his middle name, did not know how long he had been in Arizona, nor, until she received the letter, if he were alive. She wondered at the inscription and what his association had been with the hotel woman. Close enough apparently that she knew his full name.

"End of the road?"

Jerry Dillman started visibly. She had not heard him come, had thought herself all alone here, but Craig Lambert was standing back along the row when she spun around. Resentment touched her that he had startled her, then she put it down and told him, "You left the hotel so quickly. I didn't thank you for handling my trunk, for seeing that I had a room. . . ."

"No need for thanks. Anyone would help you."

"Not those loafers sprawled on the porch."

"Perhaps they're intimidated by the sterling woman who runs the hotel."

She bridled again. "I can't say anything against her. She cared for my father when he needed it most."

"What makes you so sure?"

"What does that mean?"

"Just a caution. You have only her word. She could have fired the shot that killed him herself."

"That's a horrible thing to say."

34

His eyes were steady on her. "I'm just suggesting that you might talk to some other people before you buy her story."

"Who? You and she are the only people who have shown any willingness to talk."

"I know. A town like this is pretty close-mouthed, suspicious of strangers. Most of the population of Phoenix are not here for the climate but because the law somewhere else wants them."

It was true, she knew, and unaccountably she was annoyed at him for spelling it out, and her words were sharp.

"Is that why you're here?"

He smiled. "Ma'am, will you believe I am in town because you are? Truth is, when I got on the stage at Denver I saw you and decided I had to know where you were going."

Jerry Dillman flushed, furious and uneasy alone with this man in this empty graveyard. Then the sense of humor that had rescued her before took hold and she said tartly, "You seemed to be so straightforward and now I find you are probably the greatest liar it has been my fortune to meet."

His head tipped back and he laughed, a deep throated sound welling up from his chest.

"You do come to your point directly. You don't dissemble like most people."

"You mean most women?"

"Well, since you said it, yes."

He appeared slightly disconcerted and it reassured her to put him on the defensive. She showed him an ironic smile.

"Do you really know a great deal about women, or just imagine you do?"

She broke off the talk there and walked away, out through the gap in the rock wall, and he did not follow her. She looked back once as she reached the sidewalk. He still stood where she had left him but he was not watching after her. His head was bent, his attention apparently on her father's grave.

CHAPTER 5

Jerry Dillman spent a sleepless night and it was evident by her eyes, her pale face when she came down to breakfast the next morning. Craig Lambert was just finishing and stopped by her table on his way out, sounding concerned.

"You look troubled, Miss Dillman. Anything I can do?"

"I wish I could think so." Her smile trembled a trifle. "But this isn't as simple as handling a trunk. My godfather was supposed to meet me here but he hasn't arrived. Mame Carter says I ought to go back to Denver, not to wait around and probably go broke. She doesn't think he'll come."

Without invitation Lambert sank onto the chair opposite. "Why does she think he won't show up?"

"She . . . I can't talk about it, but it's very important to me."

Lambert sat back, looking relaxed, and accepted a third cup of coffee from the waitress. When she had gone he said quietly,

"I wouldn't be too hasty then. Perhaps he's been delayed, maybe a stage breakdown. . . ."

"I hope that's it. Maybe I'd better stay a day or two . . ."

Through the following week Lambert kept her in town, offering her one hope and then another that Pop Engle would finally arrive. Mame Carter fumed that the girl should be on her way, then, finding Jerry listening to the man instead of to her, gave Jerry a job in the kitchen. Mame Carter knew all about being out of money in a strange town.

It was eight days before Pop Engle, Loco Smith and Wolf Garrison rode into Phoenix. They would have made it sooner but it had taken two days to steal horses and saddles.

They rode up before the hotel as Jerry was sweeping the blown sand off the gallery, taking pleasure in rousting the loafers for at least long enough to finish the chore. She paid no attention to the three riders until a whoop brought her head up to see a skinny old man with a long beard drop off his horse and bound toward her, shouting.

"Jerry . . . Geraldine Dillman. . . . Why, ain't you a sight for sore eyes. . . . I'm Pop Engle . . . know you wouldn't recognize your old godfather, child."

The blond girl had recoiled at the onrush. Now she dropped the broom and launched herself into his open arms, at once laughing and crying in relief.

"Pop . . . Oh . . . Where have you been? I was worried sick."

Through the effusive greeting Loco and the wolf sat their horses warily, searching the morning street for signs of danger. There was no one in sight except three nondescript men leaning against the front wall, obviously impatient to be able to sink to a comfortable crouch again and continue their mindless vigil, and another young man who idled out through the door and appeared to have no interest except in the girl. Satisfied, they turned their attention to her too. The reality was even better than the promise of the tintype. Loco Smith coughed for attention.

The girl glanced toward the mounted men and smiled. "Your friends, Pop, who are they?"

Engle, squirreling through his mind for a way to break the news that he no longer had her father's map, grabbed at the distraction to put off the telling. Leaning close to her ear he whispered.

"Loco Smith and Wolf Garrison," then added aloud. "Best friends a man could have. They rescued me from Indians that was torturing me."

Her eyes rounded, her hand went to her mouth and she swung around to the man who had eased forward to the edge of the porch.

"Craig . . . did you hear that? . . . This is my godfather, Pop Engle."

Craig Lambert had been watching the old man, watching the pair on the horses while apparently intent on the girl. He offered a hand and a nod and said amiably, "You trying to scare her with that Indian story?"

"No I ain't." Here was another chance to delay the moment of truth and he caught at it eagerly. "A pack of Mojave Apaches grabbed me. They thought I'd escaped from Yuma prison. Wouldn't believe I fell off the river boat."

Jerry Dillman gasped. "You fell overboard?"

Engle tossed a glance at the interested loafers and towed the girl down the step and to the middle of the street where his companions waited, saying reluctantly, "Well, actually I was pushed . . ."

Craig Lambert trailed idly after them and all three men put their eyes on him. Silence fell. Jerry felt the sudden tension and said hurriedly,

"This is Craig Lambert. I've been here a week and if it hadn't been for him I'd have given up and gone away. He kept telling me something had happened to hold you up. What was it?"

38

Pop Engle sighed, at the end of his evasions. He might as well tell it and have it over. He told of boarding the steamer at San Francisco and meeting Steve and Ned Albert.

"Brothers?" It was Lambert who asked.

"That's what they said. Right now I don't know what to believe. The captain knew them, said they were mining men and could be trusted. Now, I'm not as young as I was and I'd heard the Superstitions are the roughest place this side of hell. I knew we'd need help, Jerry, so I kind of broached the idea I had something good and said I'd cut them in for a third if they'd join us and put up the money for the outfit.

"They wouldn't until I'd show them the map, then they agreed. We transferred to the *River Queen* at the mouth of the Colorado and the second night Ned insisted I give him the map for security or they wouldn't pay for the outfitting at Ehrenburg, but I wouldn't go for that. The map wasn't mine, it was Jerry's. They finally said all right, but the next night they caught me up on the Texas, put a gun on me and took the map, then they threw me in the river."

Jerry Dillman groaned. Loco Smith could not tell whether it was over the loss of the map or sympathy for her godfather, then she said breathlessly, "And the Indians mistook you, but these gentlemen got you away from them." Her green eyes went up to Loco and the wolf. "Mr. Smith . . . Mr. Garrison, thank you for that."

Loco Smith felt the hairs rise at the back of his neck and Garrison growled almost inaudibly. Craig Lambert did not look away from the girl as Engle went on with his tale.

"They sure did, and it took some talking. They're freighters and the Apaches grabbed them and their wagon too. Biggest thieves in the world, the Mojaves. So there the boys were with their goods gone and nothing to do, and they agreed to come along and help catch them Alberts and get the map back."

Jerry pounced on the words with new hope. "You think we have a chance?"

"With Wolf along we do. Loco tells me that as a tracker he can follow a road runner over a granite cliff."

Craig Lambert sounded less than enthusiastic. "How much of a share in Jerry's money did you promise them?"

Pop Engle offered his hands, palms up. "They said they'd do it for anything Jerry wants to give them. That's fair, isn't it?"

Lambert raised his brows. "You'd better think it over, Jerry. You don't know anything about these people."

Engle bridled, saying angrily, "Well I know them and I say we need them. Jerry, it's your money and your decision whether or not we go get it. Me, I need a drink while you do your thinking." He swung on his heel and stalked toward the saloon entrance.

Loco Smith reached for Engle's reins and jerked his head at Garrison. "Let's go put the horses up."

They walked the animals the length of the dirt street to the livery, turned them into the hard-packed square of the corral and draped the saddles over the pole fence, then Loco pushed his flat shoulders against the top pole.

"I don't like this. That Lambert. I smell lawman. He's worn a badge and I'll bet you he still does."

Garrison said slowly, "Uh-huh. We'd better get rid of him, quick."

"Not until I know what he's up to. One thing, he knows who we are, I saw it on his face. And to cinch it that damn fool told the girl our right names."

"He isn't local. She said he rode the stage with her from Denver."

"That's it." Loco snapped his fingers. "All the way here from Denver. He's following her."

"Don't blame him for that." Wolf grinned. "The way she looks I'm tempted myself."

"That's not why, Wolf. The money she's hunting was stolen. Who takes the biggest interest in stolen money?"

"Wells Fargo."

"Now you're thinking like a real wolf. I'd say they've been keeping track of Jerry ever since her old man disappeared, figuring that sooner or later he'd get in touch with his kid and she could lead them to him. Make sense?"

Wolf was cautious. "Maybe. . . ."

"Look. Jerry gets a letter and right away sells her restaurant and takes off for this noplace. Lambert, if he is Wells Fargo, tags along after her. He probably didn't know her old man is dead or that he left a map. He's just looking for Dillman. He probably didn't know about Pop Engle until the girl told him she was to meet him here, then he kept her in town when she'd decided he wasn't coming. Now we drop in on him like a bonus. If he could take Pop and you and me in, what else could he want?"

"The money."

"You are so right. Let's go talk to Pop."

They found Engle against the bar talking with a man in a dirty apron behind it. It was early in the day and the shadowed room was otherwise empty. Pop had one hand around a bottle of whiskey and Loco frowned. All the money they had was what they had taken from the guard, Al, and they would need outfitting for the treasure hunt. Still, he felt entitled to one drink, his first as a free man. He walked with Garrison to the bar and signaled for glasses, and as the man went off down the counter Engle said in a low voice,

"The Alberts came through here ten days ago, outfitted with a spare pack mule and got a guide to take them into the mountains."

"Find out which way they went?"

"By Broken Ax Canyon."

"How do we find it?"

"Bartender's got a brother who will show us for fifty dollars."

"We need an outfit too. Fifty on top of that is more than we've got and I don't want to pull a job here, at least until we get back."

"Jerry will have some. I hope."

"What's to keep this brother from trailing us after he shows us the canyon?"

The old man winked. "I asked that. Bartender tells me his brother wouldn't go more than half a mile in there for all the gold in Mexico. He says the place is crawling with Apaches."

"I was afraid of that."

Pop said in a worried voice, "You're not backing out, are you?"

Over his head Loco and Garrison exchanged amused glances. The bartender, having loitered long enough to give Pop time to talk the matter over, brought three glasses and poured them full although no one had invited him to drink.

"Is it a deal, gents?"

Loco and Wolf both nodded and the man left again, saying, "I'll go get Sam. He's in the back room."

While he was away Pop said, "We'll be all right. We'll take that young Lambert, that gives us four guns. They say the Apaches in these parts are all bronco, sneaked away from the reservation, never more than four or five in one bunch."

Loco wished he were that confident. He was not fond of Apaches in any number. "You happen to know that Lambert character, Pop?"

The old man showed surprise. "Why would I?"

"I thought Jerry might have written you something about him."

"Nope. I never heard of him until we rode in here. What about him?"

The wolf said somberly, "We think he's wearing a badge."

"What? Why?"

"He could be a railroad detective or Wells Fargo. They may have been watching Jerry on the chance she'd lead them to Dilly Dillman."

Engle puffed out his cheeks with quick anger. "The mangy coyotes. That's like them, hiding behind a woman. I remember once in Kansas City, this redhead hanging out in the Cattleman's Bar. Come to find she was pointing out the boys who had ready money and no sign of earning it. I had to go out a back window when they started building up a posse. . . ."

Loco had enough reminiscences of his own and no time to listen to others now.

"I agree we take him. He might come in handy, and we can shoot him before we come out. That way we can blame it on the Apaches. Maybe they're good for something after all."

They were interrupted by the arrival of the bartender and his brother, a long, lank man with a drooping mustache and unhappy eyes, who was introduced as Sam Stovel. Under their questioning he said he not only knew where Broken Ax Canyon was but he had showed the way to the man who was guiding the Alberts. And he had questions of his own.

"Are you fellows lawmen going after them or what? They said they was prospectors but they didn't look like that to me. Took a pick and shovel but no gold pan and they dressed like gamblers. Then they was so all-fired secretive as to what they was up to."

"I'll tell you what," Loco said. "They're hunting the old Aztec gold but the joke's on them. They're looking in the wrong place. It's over by Santa Fe. You see, they murdered the man who had the map. That's why we're chasing them. He was my brother."

"Oh. I see."

Loco swung the subject away from reasons. "We'll start tomorrow at daylight. Pick us up at the hotel, and I'd appreciate it if you don't tell anyone in town why we're going."

"Not a soul, mister, but what about my fifty dollars?"

"See me at the hotel in an hour and I'll give you half. The rest you get when you put us in the mouth of that canyon."

Out on the street Pop Engle exploded. "What made you tell that wild yarn, Loco?"

Loco Smith shrugged, smiling. "You know Sam will talk, and if the idea gets around that we're after buried money we'd have the town sneaking along on our trail. But if it's only murderers we're looking for, the fear of Indians will keep them off our necks."

"Well I'll be," Pop wondered. "Why didn't I think up that myself?"

CHAPTER 6

At daybreak when the desert was already hot with the stored heat of past suns they lined out, south, then bearing eastward. Sam Stovel led with Jerry Dillman on one side of him, Craig Lambert on the other. Wolf rode next with Pop Engle and Loco brought up the rear with the pack mules.

It was nearly thirty miles to Apache Junction which was little more than the crossing of two trails. The country was exceedingly rough, cut into gullies and dry washes where flash floods had torn the sandy floor apart, but the rising sun rimmed the jutting peaks of the distant mountains with a glitter of gold that held out high promise.

The heat increased as the day advanced. They had to dismount and rest the animals every few miles, so it was late afternoon when they passed the junction and made a dry camp.

In Phoenix Loco and Wolf had argued earnestly that the girl had no business going on so dangerous a trip and been flatly overruled by her. With woman's logic she maintained that it was her map that had been stolen and her money that had bought the supplies, paid for the pack mules and the guide. Craig Lambert had backed her up and Pop Engle halfheartedly agreed.

"I can't blame her, Loco. I let her down once, losing the map and she wants to see for herself what happens if we get it back. If we had it we could just go to the place, get Dilly's money and clear out of here."

Wolf Garrison was doubtful. "How do we know the Alberts haven't already done just that?"

Engle sounded unhappy. "We don't. Except, I've been talking to Sam. If they had come out of the mountains they'd have come back through Phoenix and they haven't. Sam doubts they ever will."

"Indians?"

"Maybe. But the people around here didn't dream up the name Superstitions for a joke. I've heard old-timers tell some strange stories about them hills. If I believed in spirits I doubt I'd be going in there. Lots of talk that they're really haunted, men seeing strange lights and one saw a whole rock cliff burning when there wasn't a blade of grass or a sliver of wood within miles."

Loco understood. He had run into some unexplainable things himself in his travels. There is a quality about rugged mountains that makes man feel small and defenseless, uneasy in the awesome presence, and the Superstitions were reputed to be worse than most, brooding above deep, narrow canyons dark at the bottom except when the sun was directly overhead. There were said to be large waterless wastes where a man could die of thirst, eerie whistling noises made by the wind rushing down the gorges and ruins which had stood generations before the white man had come to the land. He lifted his gaze to the forbidding crags they would be entering on the following day, found them bleak to say the least and felt a tingle along his spine. Resolutely he put the qualm away. Whatever mysterious phenomena he

46

had witnessed he had not come to harm through them. It was men who had been his problem.

Sam Stovel, with the mournful eyes of a bloodhound, had a reputation as a spieler of yarns and had occupied the lonely day regaling Jerry Dillman with harrowing stories of early Indian attacks on men who had ventured into these mountains, of ghosts that haunted the canyons and caves guarding the gold that many had searched for and never found. He was still talking as he unloaded the mule and built his small supper fire.

Loco Smith watched the girl, her face bright and animated at Stovel's tales, her laugh a full-bodied peal that gave life to the otherwise empty world around them. *If I'd met a woman like that when I was young,* he thought. Loco had just passed his twenty-fourth birthday and it seemed to him that he had seen all the wickedness of which mankind was capable. He turned his head to look at Wolf Garrison, lying with his head cradled in the crook of his arm, his sharp black eyes also riveted on Pop Engle's goddaughter. Loco watched him for several minutes without the wolf taking notice, watched Garrison's tight, rigid mouth curve and twitch as though he were enjoying some secret daydream. Then the wolf felt Loco's attention, glanced at him and quickly away like a small boy caught in a forbidden area.

Loco shifted to consider Craig Lambert. The man sat with his back against a rock, his pipe clenched in his mouth as he listened to Sam Stovel, but the enigmatic face had loosened and the level, dappled hazel eyes glowed as they followed Jerry Dillman around the camp.

Fine, Loco thought. She was batting a hundred if he knew anything about odds. Two escaped convicts and a lawman of some sort. He wondered how she would react when she found out his and Wolf's background, when she discovered that instead of being interested in her personally Craig Lambert was only chasing Dilly Dillman's stolen horde. But he would never know. He would never see her again after they turned her back with the guide at Broken Ax Canyon. At least it was a pleasure to watch her having so much fun today.

Jerry Dillman was indeed having fun. She had hated the restaurant, hated the restrictions it put on her time and activities. She had always looked longingly to the great mountains above the city and had never been able to enter them.

Now she was free. There was nothing to prevent her going into the Superstitions and she looked forward to it with a child's excitement. Finding her father's money was of emotionally secondary importance.

She did know from his letter that it was a great deal but she did not know where he had gotten it or why he had felt it necessary to bury it in a remote place. She was puzzled and meant to ask Pop Engle about it when the opportunity offered, but so far there had been no chance to see him alone. There was a great deal that was curious about the whole business. Who were the two men Engle had brought with him? Was Pop lying about the map being stolen? She did not want to suspect him where her father had trusted him, but Mame Carter had doubted him from the first and Mame knew more about men than Jerry did.

Jerry had never had male friends. The men who had patronized the restaurant had been making passes since the first time she put up her hair and she had fought them off by holding herself aloof. She had discouraged Craig Lambert out of habit, but she was finding him different from the rest. He had not tried familiarity and in the few days she had known him she had discovered in him a sense of wry humor that he screened from most people by an austere shyness. He could make her laugh and there was an odd comfort in his presence. She had been surprised when he had not joined Loco and Wolf in insisting it was too dangerous for her to come on this venture, and felt a warmth toward him for his apparent faith in her capability.

Craig Lambert, too, was thinking about her being here, considering his position. He had no intention of letting her go beyond the canyon mouth. He had accepted her coming this far only because he wanted to find out what she and the three men were up to and he thought he would not be allowed to accompany them unless the girl insisted. Then Pop Engle had surprised him by inviting him along. Whatever the reason, that had alerted him to be particularly on guard.

For three years Lambert had been searching for Dilly Dillman and his partner Gilbert Engle. He was operating under the direct order of Jimmy Hume, head of the Wells Fargo detectives. Not only had Dillman held up Wells Fargo stages carrying the boxes out of Tombstone, he had had the effrontery to stop one in which Hume himself was riding and had taken the pair of pearl-handled revolvers which were Hume's pride. Furious, Hume had summoned Lambert from Montana believing that Craig would not be recognized as an agent in the south, and told him to bring Dillman and Engle to justice if it took the rest of his life.

The trail had been long and discouraging. The two outlaws had vanished from the West, so Lambert had mouse-holed Dillman's wife and after her death, the daughter. He had watched her without her becoming aware of him. He had never entered the restaurant because she might recall him later, but since he could not avoid her on the stage he had made her acquaintance as the easiest way of keeping track of her.

It had made her a suspect that he could find no male friends, nor any close female relationships in Denver. By nature and training Lambert was cynical about the honesty of most people. He had learned early that on the average honesty was only skin deep, and even those who would never steal themselves were not averse to benefiting from the larceny of others. The girl might never have considered robbery herself, but now she was going to a lot of trouble to locate the express company's money her father had stolen. It seemed improbable that she was ignorant of its source. She must have heard or read of Dilly Dillman and made an association. She might even have recognized the dodgers offering a five-thousand-dollar reward for his arrest and conviction. By her present age she must know that her father had been a notorious highwayman.

Yet looking at her now, listening to her all week, he could not convince himself of her guilt. A purity of heart shone from her like an inner light. He swore silently at himself. He was going on thirty, far too old and experienced to be moved by such a girl. He knocked out his pipe, stowed it in a pocket, saying, "That's enough lies for tonight, Sam. Jerry, let's take a walk, stretch our legs."

She turned at once from helping Stovel red the camp and Loco called a warning.

"Watch for snakes. Sidewinders like to prowl after dark."

Lambert was already cutting a greasewood pole to beat the ground ahead, then they moved away side by side.

Loco told Garrison in a low tone, "If he hurts her I'll bury him up to his neck and call in the Apaches."

"You couldn't be jealous?"

Loco grunted. "Even with my record I'm a better catch than any lawman. I wonder what old Dilly would do if he knew his girl was making eyes at one."

Garrison was gruff. "She's not making eyes at anybody. Just being polite."

From the gathering darkness her laugh floated back, gay, happy, genuine.

"That's polite? First thing a woman does when she makes a play is to laugh at a man's corny jokes." He carried his blanket away from the fire, rolled in it and lay awake, trying not to listen for the sound of Jerry Dillman's laughter.

Dilly Dillman's daughter was stargazing, watching the wide, high sky bloom with the big desert lights, filling herself with freedom and the love of life just opening up to her, hanging in delight on Craig Lambert's rambling words as he sought to entertain her.

50

"You're a bigger liar than Sam Stovel," she teased. "How could he keep the army at bay all that time?"

Lambert chuckled. "It's true. Old Owl Eye was one smart Indian. Every time they moved against him he'd go to bed and pretend he was dying. The colonel in charge of the agency got tired of the game and next time the chief pulled his act he sent troopers in to roust him out. But that was a mistake. The chief was really sick, had smallpox. Two troopers caught it and gave it to several more. They were lucky it didn't wipe out the regiment."

"You're gulling me because I'm a greenhorn," she accused. "I just don't believe you."

He sounded offhand. "That's the way it goes. Give a man a reputation and no matter what he does there are doubters who won't believe him, like a reformed stage robber, for instance. . . . Some do reform, I've heard, but it's hard to live down."

She did not rise to the bait but instead caught her breath and pointed at the full moon as it slipped quickly above the crests and poured a silver flood across the desert.

"Oh . . . Oh . . . I never saw anything so beautiful. . . ."

Lambert had to agree. The sand waste that had been terrible under the sun now lay frosted in this gentle light. The earth still sent up shimmers of heat but now the whole brutal scene was softened, looking like a reflection on water.

Craig Lambert was not a romantic and almost never impulsive, but as the girl swung with her face turned up to his in rapt ecstasy, his hands swept out, caught her shoulders and he pressed his mouth hard against hers.

It took them both by surprise. Lambert had had not the slightest idea of kissing her. Instinctively Jerry pulled back and just as instinctively Lambert held her, blurting,

"Jerry . . ."

"Please . . ."

"Listen to me. I have to say it. You can't go into those mountains tomorrow."

51

She wrenched again, shocked. "Why?"

He let her go and said in a quick burst, "It's too dangerous. Jerry, I've just found out how important you are to me. I can't risk your going there."

She stood back, bewildered. "But you didn't object when the others did. . . ."

He was silent, his teeth clamped shut because he dared not explain.

She had her own rush of words. "I am going, Craig. For the first time I feel alive. For the first time I am able to do something I want. All my life it's been, Don't do this, Don't do that. I don't know what came between my mother and father but something made her terribly bitter. I couldn't have friends come to the restaurant so I never made any friends. I couldn't go anywhere. Then she died and I was too busy trying to keep the place running to do anything except work."

"But the Superstitions . . ."

"Are adventure."

With the moon at her back he could not see her eyes but he knew they were glowing. His voice came hollow.

"The Indians, Jerry. The men we are following. The danger of thirst. . . ."

"You aren't afraid to go, are you?"

"No, but . . ."

"Then I won't stay behind. I am going wherever you go. After . . . after you touched me I wouldn't want to live if anything happened to you."

Lambert was jarred to his boot soles. The kiss had been spontaneous. He had never thought seriously of marriage. A man in his position could very seldom be at home. A Wells Fargo agent lived on the brittle brink of danger at all times.

He did not know what to say, but he did know that unless he told her the full truth he could not keep her out of the hills, and that he could not do. Suddenly he was frightened, not for himself, for her.

The odds against them were too long. It was not only danger from the Alberts who might bushwhack them, nor the Indians who could be expected hiding in the ghostly canyons. He was more afraid of what Loco Smith and Wolf Garrison might try. He knew both their reputations and even leaving Pop Engle out of consideration, if the treasure was found the two would do anything they could to keep it for themselves.

CHAPTER 7

The closer they rode to the mountain the more awesome the Superstitions appeared. There was grandeur but not beauty in the red rock that rose like giant organ pipes straight up out of the flat desert more than a thousand feet high. They hugged the cliff behind them in the lower reaches but higher they stood away from it in individual pinnacles, the tops of some balancing flat stone heads, others broken into snaggle spires. Wind, water, weather over the ages had leached the softer material out of the mountainside, washed it into mounds of rubble around the feet of the pipes, undercut the cap rock and dumped many of these to lie as great slabs tumbled on the rubble heaps. Monumental the vast hulk was, aloof, brooding, threatening as a sleeping, evil giant behind its mighty pickets.

The riders lost their voices as they approached. There was a hush over the morning. All of them felt it, a sense that they were being warned away by the demon inside the lifting ground.

Sam Stovel hunched his shoulders, pulled his head down into

them and turned it from side to side, watching the mountain face and the series of ridges that indicated canyons rising above the cliff top. Lambert, Garrison, Smith, Engle, all of them strained their eyes looking for movement, spidery figures taking up lookout positions to spy on this intrusion.

Jerry Dillman sensed the tension mounting and was thrilled by it. She had had an Indian waitress in the restaurant, a Cheyenne girl, gentle and shy and soft voiced, and she was not afraid of Indians. She had a strong suspicion that all men had a streak of Sam Stovel in them, making up stories to build their egos and impress their audiences with their bravery.

They came against the barricade of pillars and although they all looked much alike, Stovel led the party between two that were a hundred feet apart. Behind those sentries was a canyon floor, almost flat and straight for half a mile. For as far as they could see it was contained between sheer bluffs as high as the spires. This first knee of the mountain was a mesalike plateau.

Loco Smith rode at Wolf Garrison's side and gave him an uneasy look. "This is a dandy place to get caught if it happens to rain higher up. A real water chute."

Garrison was uncomfortable himself and he said, only half joking, "Might be a good time to call on that Great Spirit of yours again, ask him to see it don't rain until we get past here."

There was no more said until they reached the end of the flat floor. The canyon made a bend there and began climbing toward the plateau and a second draw branched off from it at another angle. Stovel reined in and waited until the others came up, then said in a low voice, almost a whisper,

"This one on the right is Broken Ax and it goes up a good piece, then you take your pick of where you ride. I don't go no farther."

Jerry heard fear in the tone and had a moment of panic herself. Sam was the only one here who knew any of the paths of the Superstitions and one canyon must lead into another to make a maze. If they got lost they might be weeks working their way out. Already, the draw on the right that Sam said they should take was not the main canyon which she would have chosen. She said impulsively, "Sam, how much will it take to get you to stay and guide us?"

He squinted at her. "How much will it take for one of you people to tell me what this is really about? You hinted you was after some killers, but what's a woman doing on a manhunt?"

"I'll tell you if you'll go with us. . . ."

He cut her off. "No chance, ma'am. I got out of here once with my scalp half off. One more second and that Injun would have had it all. I did some fast praying and swore on all the Bibles I ever heard of that if the good Lord would reach down and pull me out of this hell—pardon me, but that's just what it is—I'd never, never go farther than this in here again. He did and I'm keeping my promise."

This would be as big a lie as she had heard from him so far and she tried again. "Even if it gave you a chance to pick up a small fortune?"

Loco sucked in his breath. If she kept on she'd have everybody in New Mexico Territory swarming over them. Craig Lambert coughed loudly. It was going to be hard enough if they did locate the Wells Fargo treasure to get it away from the present company without having to run the gauntlet of every outlaw north of the border. But the girl had already rushed on, telling Stovel, "My father hid a lot of money back in here and we have to find the Alberts to get my map back. They stole it."

The guide's eyes narrowed. He looked from one to the other of the men as though he were weighing their chances of finding a treasure and bringing it out alive. All except the old one looked like people who had known a lot of danger and were still around to take another risk. Furthermore the way Garrison and Smith were watching him gave him the idea that they might not let him go back now that he knew what they were after. He wished to hell he hadn't asked. He wished his nose was not so long because what he had asked for was a shot in the back as soon as he turned it. Or maybe the girl could save him. Three of these men were in love with her and the other was her godfather, and just possibly that would hold them off from murder with her looking on.

He said as earnestly and urgently as he knew how, "I wouldn't go with you for a whole million dollars, ma'am, and I ain't going to let you go either. Innocent like you are you got no idea what you'd be riding into. You turn that horse around and come out of here with me."

Before she could say anything more Craig Lambert laid one hand over hers and squeezed it tightly in his own urgency.

"Do that, Jerry. It will only make it harder for us to have to watch over you. It really is too dangerous. Go back to Phoenix and wait for us. Do it because I ask you."

Wolf Garrison said in a dire tone, "That's real good advice, honey. If we run up against an Apache war party I sure wouldn't like them to get hold of you."

Loco Smith's voice was equally warning. "You must have heard what they do with white women, haven't you? Especially pretty yellow-haired ones like you. We just can't be responsible for anything like that happening. I'd never be able to live with my conscience. I'd just have to turn this gun on myself."

Pop Engle chimed in with his strenuous argument. Whatever was going to come about he was certain it would involve gun play or knife play. If they found that money all three others would try to grab it and he had no intention of letting them rob him of it. He would share it with Dilly's daughter but not by a damn sight with anybody else.

They were a human wall standing against her. It occurred to her that this was a decision she could not win. In Garrison's eyes she saw that he would forcibly tie her to her horse and send her off, and the others would probably help him. Letting her shoulders droop she said in a sad, defeated tone, "I did so want the fun of seeing Daddy's fortune where he buried it. I never knew him and it would be sort of like meeting him. But if all of you think I'll be so much trouble to you, all right, I'll go with Sam."

She heard the combined sigh of relief and did not smile, but turned her horse without a good-by and drove back toward the mouth of the canyon as though her heart would break. Sam Stovel made a hurried turn, wanting to keep as close to her as possible until he was out of the range of the guns, but Wolf Garrison's hard voice stopped him cold.

Garrison put his horse close to Stovel's and looked into the guide's face for a long silent moment, then he glanced to where the girl had stopped to wait for the man, and sighed.

"It goes against my better judgment to let you ride out of here alive now, but I wouldn't want her to see me put a hole through you. Take her to town and watch over her good. And if I find out you've opened that yap of yours about her money to anybody at all there's no place you can run to that I won't find you. I'll cut your wagging tongue out and make you eat it."

Stovel's eyes rolled in his relief. The good Lord had rescued him from this place again and he said a silent promise that he would never come even this far into the Superstitions, ever.

"I ain't going to say one word and you can make book on it, Mr. Garrison. I like my tongue where it is, and besides I wouldn't want to do anything that might hurt that little girl any ways at all."

"Clear out then before I change my mind," the wolf growled.

Stovel wheeled his animal and spurred it down the passage, not feeling safe until he reined in beside the girl. He was far enough away then that he doubted they would fire for fear of hitting her. Not until they were outside the pillars once more did he remember that he had not been paid the second half of the fifty dollars he had been promised, but that was a sacrifice he would gladly make. Maybe though he could talk Jerry Dillman into paying him. He would work on that during their ride.

The men sat where they were until the pair was out of sight, growing conscious of the eerie stillness of the hills. There was not the scuttle of a rodent, the cry of a bird, the rattle of slipping stones. When they could no longer see the slight blond figure they turned to each other, appraising. Craig Lambert understood clearly that both Loco and Garrison were weighing the wisdom of gunning him down here and now and raised his eyes to the brutal slopes above them and let a touch of fear come through his voice.

"Feels like there isn't a soul within a hundred miles, doesn't it? But we know the place is crawling. Carney, who killed Jerry's father is supposed to have come in here to look for the money. . . . The Alberts and their guide . . . Apaches probably looking at us from up there right now. You think the four of us can handle them all?"

That little speech saved his life. Loco shrugged.

"One way to find out is to get started. I don't like the idea of staying in here any longer than I have to, so let's go find the Alberts and that map."

"If they're still alive." Lambert drove home as deeply as he could the dangers ahead because only as long as they believed his guns were needed against a force of unknown strength would he have a chance of surviving. "As many days ahead of us they are, the Indians may already have made buzzard bait of them."

Wolf Garrison was getting the message and Pop Engle showed some signs of nervousness, but Loco Smith laughed suddenly.

"Let's not get all spooked before we've got a reason. I'd say between us we can manage what we have to and if the Alberts are dead they're dead, but if they aren't I want to know it."

He swung his horse out of the main canyon into the smaller one where the tracks of a previous party of horsemen were clear. Obviously whoever they were they had not expected to be followed. If it was the Alberts they would believe Pop Engle had either not escaped the currents of the Colorado or had fallen into the hands of the Mojave Apaches and in either case would pose no threat to them.

Broken Ax Canyon proved to be a twisting, tortuous grade that wound higher and higher and the tracks climbed one side of it along a narrow ledge, the ground falling away in a steep drop to a bottom too choked with broken boulders to use as a trail. One of Sam Stovel's campfire stories had been of the way it got its name. Some forgotten man had been exploring here and thought he was the first white man to discover the long draw until he topped out of it and found an ax with a broken handle stamped MADE IN BIRMINGHAM, ENGLAND.

Barrel and saguaro cactus grew sparsely in the rocky ground and greasewood clung in the dry rills where its deep roots reached far down to underground water. There was very little other vegetation on the sun-wracked land.

Wolf Garrison took the lead, riding far enough in advance that he could hear it if there was any sound to betray another presence, warn him of an ambush. Loco took the rear position, sitting backward in his saddle. Uncomfortable as it was he did not want the wily Apaches to let the train pass, then drop in behind them where they could be trapped between those below and others above.

A mile up the draw his horse stopped without his command and he twisted his head to see why. The other horses were standing still and at the head of the column Wolf Garrison was off his animal, beckoning to the others and climbing the stiff bank. Loco looked to where the wolf was headed and saw a mound of earth recently disturbed, obviously dug into. Wolf fell on his knees, calling,

"Cover me, Loco. I think we've found it."

Loco swung in his saddle, yanking his rifle from the boot and leveling it at Lambert and Engle while Garrison clawed with his hands in the loose earth. He threw grit between his knees like a burrowing badger until he was elbow deep, then he sat back and called in disgust.

60

"Nothing down there and it hasn't been dug below. Ground's hard as stone."

Engle chuckled but did not explain. Loco put the rifle away in bitter disappointment.

"That mean the Alberts already found the money and cleared out?"

Garrison scratched at his head, looking uphill with a shrug. "If they did why did they keep on going up?"

"We'd better find out. We might still come up with them."

The train got under way again and in the next five miles found three more empty cairns.

"What are they? What do they mean?" Loco was completely puzzled.

"That's Dilly's way," Pop Engle told them. "His little joke. He was mighty secretive about money and he had a devious way of thinking. He'd have brought it with him on his pack animals and been afraid somebody might trail him, see him bury it and go in and get it after he'd gone away."

Gilbert Engle remembered well how his partner had effectively hidden both shares of their early money to start their freight line with, had kept him on an allowance until Wells Fargo had ruined them and they had gone on their private warpath.

"What he did was leave these false leads to be dug up, then he went and put his funds in some entirely different place. We just have to run them Alberts down."

By the noon stop the intense stillness had not been broken except by their fruitless investigation of other deceptive mounds and slides of rock that only whetted their appetites. There were no other noises. There was no movement other than theirs to be seen. Garrison chose a spot where the trail looped into a shallow draw and there was a little nearly level ground, dismounted but left the horse saddled and ready in case it should be needed in a hurry and cut greasewood branches for a small coffee fire.

61

"What the hell you doing?" Pop Engle objected. "A fire's going to tell any Indian for a mile around where we are."

"Naw." The wolf built his pile of twigs, very disgruntled. "Not unless they're downhill and we'd have been jumped if they were. Downdraft will take the smell and the smoke that way. Get down and give your animal a rest. There's a lot more hill to climb today."

They spent an hour there relaxing but watchful, then went on. Before sunset they were on a bench from the back of which rose a sheer wall high enough that even Apaches could not drop on their heads and a flat rock floor stretched an eighth of a mile on either side. They could not be surprised except from below where the trail came around a sharp bend and to the bench at a grade the horses could barely lurch up.

Again Garrison made the supper fire where the wind would blow the telltale odor down. He put the coffeepot on while Loco stirred a pan of biscuits and put chili con carne already cooked to heat. The plates had been dished up and the four of them sat cross-legged on the rock. Loco had a forkful halfway to his mouth when the sound came. Definitely hoofs clicking on stone down below.

There was a scramble, plates set aside, guns drawn, and they scattered, back away from the edge, crouching in the open, fingers on their triggers, waiting for the first savage head to appear.

Garrison said in a low tone, "Only one horse. Could be Carney?"

"Maybe, or maybe an Albert. But what are any of them doing behind us, coming this way?"

"Apache?" Pop Engle's voice was tight.

Loco shook his head. "The horse is wearing iron."

The animal appeared in a sudden strong lunge up the bank and Engle fired. Some instinct made Lambert jump and knock the old man's gun up just as he squeezed and the bullet went into the air.

The horse was still scrambling for footing when they saw the rider, a blond head with her hat hanging against the back of her neck, leaning forward in her stirrups to help the animal's balance. When it stood solidly on top Jerry Dillman swung down and smiled from one to the other.

Craig Lambert groaned under his breath. Pop Engle yelped his fright that he had nearly shot her. Loco and the wolf froze in shock. Lambert found his voice first, almost a cry.

"What are you doing here for God's sake?"

Garrison growled, "Where's that son of a . . . 'scuse . . . Stovel? Why didn't he hold onto you?"

Jerry shook her hair back and said brightly, "His horse sprained a leg and he had to walk and I just had to come. It's so important to me."

Loco Smith sounded strangled. "You've been on this trail all day . . . alone . . . ? You crazy, stupid damn fool. The least that could have happened to you was to get yourself lost . . . How did you find us?"

"I knew which way you started, then after a while I smelled your camp fire and just followed my nose. That's not bad for a tenderfoot, is it?"

The men looked at each other in helplessness. She was here, a fact that had to be accepted. None of them wanted it but neither did they know how to get her out of the mountains again. They could not send her down alone. One of them could take her but which one would give up the hunt? Which would let the others go on and find the hundred thousand dollars and be long gone with it before he could return?

Loco Smith decided that behind that beguiling face there was a very sly mind. She had it all figured out. They would take her along because they had to and it put him in a very tight spot. When the money was found he would have to think of some very fancy moves to get rid of these other people before he could take her and the money out of these hills.

Wolf Garrison and Engle were thinking the same thing and

Craig Lambert saw the job of taking the horde and any prisoners back to Phoenix made much more difficult if not impossible.

Their displeasure was like something solid hanging in the air. For the first time the shiver of a qualm ran through her and made her eyes widen into round blue moons. She did not really know any of these men and there was now a hardness about their mouths that she was sure had not been there before. What it betokened she did not know. But ever since the ride had begun she had been aware of their attention and she knew the three younger ones were much interested in her as a woman. If they were interested enough she could only hope that each would protect her from the others.

In her childhood her mother had been courted by men, always two, three or four at once. There had never been a single suitor, and it came to Jerry here that this had been deliberate on her mother's part. In this moment of high awareness she understood why, understood that she would have to take care in keeping a delicate balance in how she behaved with each of these. She dropped her eyes and like a guilty child led her horse to where the others were picketed, hobbled it and hauled the saddle off.

For the first time on this trip no one moved to do the chore for her. She had even been amused that there appeared to be a rivalry over who would do the most for her. Now she was being punished, and the only thing she knew to do was to accept it, make herself useful wherever she could, not be a burden to them.

They were stiffly silent when she went to the fire, their attention on their plates as though each one was absorbed in his own thoughts to the exclusion of anything else. She brought her plate from her saddlebag and dished a little chili onto it, not much although she had not had anything to eat at noon and she was hungry, but it was a way of showing she did not want to take from them what they had intended as their supper.

64

Afterward she cleaned the utensils and stowed them as she had watched Sam Stovel do, then spread her blanket at the base of the cliff and rolled in it although the sky was still light.

She listened to their low talk, unable to hear the words but knowing by the tones there was an argument. Much later, when the moon was high, she heard them moving and turned over to watch.

Craig Lambert took his blanket ten feet to her right and lay down there. Loco Smith took his ten feet to her left and stretched out. Pop Engle curled up between her and the lip of the shelf and Wolf Garrison sat down, his legs folded under him, facing the spot where the trail came up, his rifle across his lap and his short gun unholstered on the ground close to his hand. The wolf did not expect an Apache raid during the night—they were not normally night fighters—but there was a chance of one if they had seen the blond girl.

The more Wolf thought about her being here the madder he got. He had tried to talk Loco and the lawman into escorting her downhill. He and the old man would have been short handed but if they stayed in this spot they would be fairly secure and he had promised to do that until they could catch up with Stovel, turn the girl's horse over to the guide and start them riding double for town. Craig Lambert had been willing. Wolf guessed that the man had an idea that once the girl was safe he could throw down on Loco and capture him, stake him out somewhere and then come up the canyon again. Garrison did not believe any one man could take Loco, but the question was moot. Loco Smith absolutely refused to turn back, and considering the wolf's history he did not really blame him. His word had never been the most trustworthy. Lambert would not go alone, which Wolf considered glaring proof that the money and his and Loco's hides were most important to him. He was not along just for the ride. It was the neatest Mexican standoff Wolf had ever seen.

There was no disturbance during the night. Loco Smith

spelled Garrison as guard at midnight and Lambert took over at four. They did not ask Engle to take a shift because of his age and the day had been hard on him. They did not want him collapsing at least until they had the map. Wolf and Garrison had talked it over and decided that it must be written in some code shared by Pop and his dead partner, or why else would Engle think the Alberts might not yet have found the hiding place, picked up the treasure and dodged out of the country.

In the morning they climbed again, Wolf out ahead, Loco at the rear with Lambert keeping close to Jerry Dillman. The trail went west along the shelf to a watershed break in the cliff that had worn it down to a long slope where they had to walk and lead the horses. That took them to the top of a stony ridge and they looked down the far side on a tangle of gorges and bluffs, of more ridges, one beyond another climbing the high side of the mountain bulk.

Wolf followed the clear tracks, but farther on he scouted for animal signs that would lead him to water. There was water in the Superstitions, in all of the barren Western ranges, but you had to know how to look for it. Near noon he found a little sump where mud was dried and cracked and the marks of small claws and dragging tails were etched into the hard surface.

He stopped the train there, got down and went back to the pack horse behind Loco, unlashed the shovel and pick and returned to the sump, saying, "We'll take a break here, rest the horses and fill the canteens."

Jerry Dillman dismounted and hobbled her animal. Lambert had saddled for her in the morning but no one had spoken to her all day. She walked to stand near Garrison and watch as he swung the pick at the ground that resisted like concrete. The dull red-brown substance had been dry a long time.

Wolf hacked at the crust, breaking it out in chunks from a two-foot circle, shoveling that debris away, then picking out another layer. By the time he was down a foot the digging was

66

easier and in another six inches moisture changed the color. Dampness began to show and a warm, moist smell rose. Two feet down the mud was soft. Wolf shoveled that out and below it thick water seeped in. He bored on down and at the three-foot depth the seep was faster. The level of the soupy mix rose until the shovel blade was covered with it and the wolf used the handle to boost himself out of the hole.

Jerry Dillman wanted the silence against her broken and said in a marveling tone, "I wouldn't have believed there was a drop of water down there. How in the world did you guess?"

He said without smiling, "I didn't guess."

"You knew? But how? Is it under the whole place?"

The temptation to show off was too much for Wolf Garrison. He wiped his sleeve across the sweat on his face and pointed up the canyon wall above the hole.

"Look up there. See that break? That was cut out by water. Now, with what little rain there is here, there wouldn't be enough run-off at any one time to make that track, so it must be there's a reservoir caught under this ridge. It gets filled up and spills over when the summer flash floods hit this country."

Jerry was openly admiring, almost breathless in her next question. "But what made you notice it in the first place?"

His grin came then and he took her arm, led her down along the trail beyond the horses, crouched on his haunches and put his finger beside a faint print.

"That deer track is headed toward the sump. It told me to look sharp. Deer can always find water."

"I can hardly see it even when you show it to me. . . . Whatever could a deer find to eat in these mountains?"

Garrison stood up and reached into a crack between the rocks where a handful of brittle dry grass hung like an old man's beard.

"Most nutritious grass there is, nature cured. This and all kinds of desert flowers jump up right after a rain. They grow mighty fast while the ground's wet, and every place you find grass you find deer."

Jerry almost batted her eyes at the man. "I think it's wonderful that you know all these things. I never imagined them."

Wolf Garrison glowed. Watching him as he got a cold meal ready, Loco Smith glowered. He might still be put out that she was here but he did not like her making eyes at the wolf. He had plans about that girl himself. He did not like the sickly grin on Garrison as they passed him on the way back to spring the wolf had made, nor the hand Jerry Dillman had on the man's arm as if she needed support to walk.

The water had cleared somewhat. Wolf filled a cup carefully without disturbing the roil below the surface, strained the dark liquid through his bandana to remove the worst of the grit and passed it to the girl.

"It ain't the sweetest you ever tasted, but it's water. Drink it fast and it won't be too bad."

She swallowed it and choked, making a face. The mud taste was strong and there was a faint flavor of whiskey from the cup. But it was wet and very welcome on this parched mountain with the sun blazing on her.

After the party had each had a drink and had eaten the water was clearer. Wolf filled all the canteens, then led the horses one at a time to the spring, letting them drink sparingly.

The heat was intense, the air shimmering, hot enough to rise visibly, creating the effect that they were looking through a water veil. They rested there through the worst of the afternoon, Pop Engle asleep and snoring with ragged rasps. Loco Smith, concerned about him, soaked his blanket in the muddy hole and rigged a tent of it so a damp breeze and shade might help him. Craig Lambert made one like it for Jerry and a third that he and Loco and Wolf took turns under while two stood watch.

By four-thirty the red ball in the sky had sunk behind the mountain. They mounted and strung out again through the heat that still reflected off the rock.

CHAPTER 8

For three days they pushed higher into the deep reaches of the Superstitions, hearing nothing, seeing no one. There had been no water and Loco had had his turn at being the hero, cutting the heads off thick barrel cactus and scooping out the pulp where the plant stored moisture. Chewing that pulp had saved many a life in the deserts. And the girl was satisfyingly impressed.

Throughout those three days there had been no more of Dilly Dillman's mocking mounds. The hills could be empty of human life, even of the ghosts that frightened so many men. There were no burning walls of rock except as the sun heated them to oven temperatures, no shrieks of wind except the drafts that whined down the tortured gorges, no Apaches.

About those Loco said in growing anxiety, "Where are they? You know they're in here and I've been feeling them watching us, but what are they doing? What are they waiting for? I'm getting tired of holding my breath."

"I don't know." The wolf sounded baffled. "Maybe they've all gone to a powwow down near the reservation. Maybe they're making medicine with one of those prophets of a messiah. I'll be pleased if they are and if they stay there until we get out."

"And where the hell are the Alberts? It doesn't make good sense that Dillman would have hauled as heavy a load as he was packing all this way. I smell something wrong."

They were waiting out another sweltering afternoon. Falling more and more under Jerry Dillman's spell the men had forgotten their anger with her and made her a mascot, a situation that could last only until the money was found or proven lost. She had no idea of the warfare that would explode then, gave it no thought, serene in the fact that she had been wholly safe this far, and now that Dillman's name had been brought up she took the opportunity to ask Engle about him.

"Tell me about my father, Pop. What kind of a man was he? How did he get all that money? Why did he hide it?"

Engle's eyes narrowed on her and all expression wiped from his face. Without a word he walked away and lay down in the shade of a rock upthrust where the horses were tied. She watched after him, bewildered.

"What do you suppose is the matter with him?"

Lambert said softly, "Maybe he doesn't want to talk about a dead man."

"Why not? Unless he knows something bad about him? And if there is I ought to know it. Suppose there is something . . . wrong . . . about his money? I wonder if Loco and Wolf know."

Torn inside Lambert watched her go quickly to where the pair was keeping a vigil of the land around them, watched the smiles they turned on her, like mountain cats with a lamb between them while they shook their heads at her questions. He was still not sure of her innocence. It could be a crafty act to use him, Garrison and Smith in a plan arranged with Gilbert

Engle. He was, after all, her godfather. In love he might be but the doubt still haunted him that she could be this ignorant of Dillman's reputation. He had known other women who had hidden criminality with convincing guile, had arrested some and seen them drop the masks and become more dangerous than any man.

But if she were all she seemed, she was the one in danger by trusting Loco and Wolf. He brooded whether to tell her who they were, that her father and Gilbert had collected the money by robbing stages. If he did he would also have to confess his own role here and she would surely accuse him of playing her along only to get his hands on the money. The hell of it was, it had begun that way and how could he convince her that was no longer all of it?

He had still not decided when Wolf and Loco brought the girl back to where he sat, Jerry looking downcast, saying,

"They didn't know my father, they only met Pop Engle a couple of weeks ago."

"We know something else though," Loco announced. "The Alberts are lost. They swung in a big circle. That No Shoes Johnson must be some guide."

That took Jerry's mind off her father for a while and she laughed. "Sam Stovel told me about him while we were riding out. Three years ago he was asleep in the cabin at his little ranch ten miles out of Phoenix when he thought he heard Apaches breaking in. He jumped out the window and ran barefoot for town and it was months before he got all the cactus out of his feet. Sam also said he doesn't know anything about these mountains but that he'd never admit it and he thought he could follow my father's trail."

"Anyway," Loco decided, "following them is the only way we're ever going to turn them up, so let's get about it."

The sun had set for them but the sky was still bright and the shade a hundred and twenty. Wiry and tough as he was, Gilbert Engle's strength was failing. Riding behind him Loco Smith wondered if the old man was going to hang on long enough. He was beginning to wilt himself, his mind wandering away from caution to the days in Yuma prison, and bad as it had been he thought it compared favorably with the Superstitions. Muddy and foul-tasting, the Colorado had at least supplied an abundance of water. The Colorado. To dive into it right now would be . . .

A low warning whistle from Garrison snapped him back to the present. He kicked his horse ahead to where the others were gathering and the wolf was pointing down at the trail. The horseshoe tracks here were overlaid with the threat they had been expecting. Moccasin prints following the earlier riders.

Loco looked from them to the bleak slopes around them. "Your powwow's over," he told Garrison. "Miss Jerry Dillman, there really are Apaches. You keep your eyes peeled from here on and if you see so much as a twig shake you say so."

He had not been aware that his alertness had flagged as uneventful day had succeeded uneventful day but now his eyes and ears seemed to leave his body and go seeking through the empty-looking land. Rifles in their hands now they moved on, the wolf well ahead. He was out of sight around a bend when his shout came back to them.

"Lambert, keep Jerry where she is. Loco, come here."

Loco put his horse at a lope around the bend and Pop Engle threw the lines of the pack animals at Lambert and pushed after Smith.

In the trail at Garrison's feet a body lay face up.

It was naked, the face eaten away by buzzards, much of it gnawed at by predators but also mutilated by knives. A pattern carved on the chest was still discernible. Clothes were scattered on the ground, a frock coat, a ruffled shirt, an elaborately patterned vest, trousers and boots with scrolls burned into the tops. The condition of the corpse and the stench that hung heavy around it indicated it had lain here two to three days.

"Ghost Dance," Wolf Garrison said in a shaken tone.

"Yeah." Loco Smith repeated to himself. "There really are Apaches."

Pop Engle had one glance for the body, then his attention went to the clothes. "That's one of them," he said in excitement. "Steve Albert. Them fancy duds sure had me fooled."

Loco Smith was also interested in the garments, getting down, fixing his bandana over his nose and methodically searching through pockets and wallet for a map while Gilbert held his horse.

The animals were trembling, shying, hard to control. Wolf Garrison yanked his down as it reared and walked it past the body along the edge where the trail skirted a drop off into a deep ravine and rode ahead, studying the ground, reading the story in the welter of tracks.

Craig Lambert put his horse far enough around the bend to see what was ahead, blocking the girl behind him and she said uncertainly, "What is it?"

"A dead man."

She crowded up beside him and he caught her rein to hold her back, but she spurred the animal and jumped it forward.

"I have to see."

He thought, perhaps she should. She was taking all the threatened perils of these mountains much too lightly and a shock like this should convince her how real they were.

Loco's horse danced in a circle, pulling Gilbert around with it and for a moment Jerry Dillman had a full view of the ugly scene. She sat frozen. The torn, bloated thing lay only eight feet from her. Every detail was branded in her brain. A scream came, involuntary, high and long and was cut off as she fainted. Craig Lambert was waiting, already out of his saddle, reaching to catch her, carry her back and lay her on the ground.

Wolf Garrison reached them first, spurring in and yanking his horse up at the turn, his face hot with indignation, cursing Lambert. The girl had had a much deeper effect on him than he had known until this second.

73

"Why the hell did you let her see?" he yelled. "I ought to put a bullet in your head."

He had already snapped the rifle up. Craig Lambert had flipped the gun from his holster. Then both of them stopped as though they had been turned to stone. If they had not needed it until now, from here on every hand and every gun available could be important. One less could cost the lives of everyone. Particularly that of Jerry Dillman. Garrison let the rifle sag. Lambert dropped the short gun in its leather and said as calmly as he could, "She didn't believe. Now she will. Give me your canteen."

Wolf Garrison got down, unslung the canteen but did not hand it to Lambert. He knelt beside the still form, wet his handkerchief and gently rubbed it over the white face. Lambert was at her other side chafing her hands and arms.

Loco Smith had heard the scream and Garrison's yell and caught his breath, expecting gunfire in the next second. When it did not come he let the air out in a low whistle. He did not go down where they worked over Jerry until he had picked up Albert's wrist, dragged him to the edge and rolled him off. The stink would linger but the blond girl would not have to look at the man again. He did not wait to see it land two thousand feet below but took his rein from Gilbert, fought the horse to quiet and then followed the old man around the bend.

Jerry Dillman's eyes were open but glazed, her head lying on Lambert's folded knee, Garrison holding the canteen against her lips to dribble water into her mouth. Loco wanted to take her away from them, hold her in his own arms, feel the soft body cling against him for comfort, but that would have to wait. Somebody had to watch that they were not jumped by Indians themselves and he did not trust Pop Engle's eyesight.

Half an hour later the girl had recovered, still pale and shaking but sitting up propped against a rock asking weak questions.

"Why did they cut him that way? Was it just to torture him?"

"More than that," Lambert said in a quiet tone, knowing that only the truth would release her from grisly speculations. "It is a religious symbol used in the Ghost Dance. Several years ago a medicine man appeared in one of the northern tribes, claiming the Great Spirit had sent him to rescue them from the white men. He told them to join in an uprising of all the tribes to drive the whites out of their lands, to kill them and mark them so the Great Spirit would know they were obeying him and raise the armies of all the dead Indians to fight with them. The word spread all through the West and nobody knows how many tribes are practicing the rites. We do know these Apaches are."

She looked at the hills, wildness in her eyes. "They're around here now?"

"Not now," Wolf Garrison said. "They ambushed the Albert party, killed the one man and took the other two prisoner, took the horses and pack animals on up this trail. No telling how far, but that's why we haven't seen them before."

Craig Lambert made his decision almost without thought. With a sweep of his hands his guns were out and trained on Smith and Garrison and his tone was blunt.

"This is enough. We are going to turn around and take her out of here. Now."

Loco Smith looked from the guns to Garrison and said mildly, "I don't think we are, Wolf, do you?"

Wolf Garrison's grin was twisted. "I don't believe we will, Loco. There's only six or seven of them, little bunch of broncos I'd say."

"Pop and Wolf and I can take them, Lambert. You ride her out if you want. We're getting close to that map and you wouldn't want to see her lose her money because of a handful of varmints, would you?"

Craig Lambert debated without relaxing. To come this close to finding the Wells Fargo cache and with some chance of taking these outlaws back, alive or dead made it imperative that he should go on with the hunt. If Garrison was telling the truth about the number of Apaches they should be no problem for four men. But the thought of even one Indian getting to Jerry Dillman turned his stomach cold. Her safety now outweighed every other consideration.

He said swiftly, "All right. I'll take her alone."

He was putting the guns away when Pop Engle's rifle barrel slammed against the back of his head and Lambert dropped, not knowing when his face hit the ground.

"Pop . . ." It was a cry from the girl and she sprang up, clawing at the old man, godfather or no, in instinctive reaction to his clubbing Lambert.

Loco caught her from behind, pulled her off and wrapped his arms around her. It was not really necessary but it was his first opportunity to do it with an excuse that would keep Garrison from butting in. She pivoted in the embrace, not trying to break it, too indignant to realize she was there, and her voice was furious.

"Why should he do a thing like that, Loco?

Smith smiled down on her hungrily. "Why don't you ask him? I wouldn't know."

"I had to, honey, just had to," Gilbert sounded apologetic. "The durn fool take you down this trail by himself, who's to say these Injuns up here are the only ones ramming around this country. He could get you killed. And another thing, I don't cotton to trying to get our map out of those red devils' hands with nobody to look after you while we're doing it. When he wakes up he's going with us, and don't you be scared. It'll all be all right."

"But you hurt him. He's bleeding . . . Loco, let me go. He needs help."

Loco turned her loose and he and the wolf watched her rush to the lawman, kneel and cradle his head in her lap, his bloody face against her legs. The two partners' eyes locked. When . . . if . . . they had the money and were safely down the mountain

76

Lambert would have a fatal accident, but neither Wolf nor Loco liked what they saw here. It was going to give whoever got her a big problem to change her mind without drastic means.

CHAPTER 9

Consciousness returned to Craig Lambert slowly. His eyes fluttered open and the sky wheeled dizzily around him. His head throbbed with a painful pulse and his face burned where the rocks had scraped his skin raw. Then a hat brim moved in close above him and Loco Smith said cheerfully, "Here he comes. Lie still, Lambert, while I patch you up."

Loco had the crushed pulp of a thick succulent leaf in his fingers, dabbing it against the cuts and scratches. Lambert raised a hand and gingerly felt the side of his head. Another leaf was tied against the gash with his bandana, its skin cut off and the slimy inner flesh was cool, soothing.

Loco would just as soon the patient died and the ministrations were for the benefit of Jerry Dillman only and he smiled at her as he explained.

"Aloe is the best healer in these parts. Cures cuts and warts quicker than anything I know. They say the Spanish brought it to America and the Mexicans and Indians moved it north.

His face will be good as new tomorrow and the place where Pop opened his scalp will close clean in a few days."

Lambert said through stiff lips, "Why did he do it?"

Jerry spoke from his other side in an anxious voice. "He meant well, Craig. He was afraid that if we went off alone other Indians would find us. I think we'd better stay together."

Lambert sat up too fast and caught at Loco's arm to keep from tumbling forward, but his voice was stronger and harsh. "You mean to take her into an Indian fight with you? Over my dead body you will." His free hand slapped at his holster and found it empty. Both guns had been taken while he was out.

Loco pushed him down again more gently than he would without the girl there. "Farthest thing from my mind, mister. When we find them you're going to stay with her until it's over. But it's too late today to go any farther, it will be dark in half an hour and we don't want to go stumbling around blind, lose the trail or run into their camp. So get a rest and you'll be able to ride by morning."

In this condition Craig Lambert knew that he could not possibly take the girl anywhere away from either the outlaws or the Indians. All that was left to him was to regain as much strength as he could to protect her through whatever lay ahead.

"I'll be able to ride. I'll be able to shoot. But if I'm going to be any good to anybody I need my guns. Where are they?"

Wolf Garrison came into Lambert's range of vision holding Craig's two guns toward him by the stocks, chuckling. The desire to shoot him was in the wolf's eyes and he held back solely because they still needed him. Lambert took hold of the barrels, flipped them in his hands and by the time he caught the butts Garrison's gun was out and leveled.

"Just in case that bump knocked your brains loose," he said.

Craig Lambert's voice despised the outlaw. "Save your ammunition for Apaches, Garrison, and you know as well as I do that a shot here could bring them down around us in minutes."

He holstered the guns and lay flat against the ground, his

strength used up by the surge of his fear for Jerry Dillman, closing his eyes to shut out the sight of mountains that again turned in slow rolls in his vision. He heard Smith and Garrison move off, then the girl was whispering close to his ear.

"What have they got against you, Craig? They're acting like they don't trust you. Why?"

In his weakened state he was on the verge of telling her the whole truth, then long training took over to stop him. He could not foresee what her reaction would be and the situation was growing critical. If she took it into her lovely, inexperienced head to confront them she would undoubtedly get him killed, and that would leave her prey for whatever they chose to do with her. He would almost as soon see her used by the Indians as by these two predatory animals. In his view there was no shred of honor toward a woman in either of them.

"They're just edgy, not knowing where the Indians are. Everybody looks like an enemy just now. Leave them alone. Stay away from them, don't get into an argument with any of them. Don't criticize Engle. Keep calm and do whatever they tell you tonight."

His voice trailed off and in the next moment Jerry knew he was asleep. She sat where she was beside him, wondering about him. None of these men talked about themselves, but that she supposed was typical, their way of not bragging. Mame Carter had warned her against all men, but maybe the hotel woman had had a bad marriage as her mother had, and certainly she had no cause for complaint about these people. They were doing all they could to help her and making every effort to please and protect her. She felt grateful to all of them and she was particularly fond of Craig Lambert. In fact when she had seen him struck down a very strong emotion had raced through her. She thought it must be love but she wasn't sure. She had never been in love.

Her godfather was sitting at the edge of the trail leaning against the canyon wall, looking much more frail than when

80

they had started the ride. The constant heat was taking a lot out of him and she was worried whether he could keep going without exhausting himself.

Loco was making a cold supper because he no longer dared risk a fire and Wolf was at the bend standing guard. Loco brought her a plate and her canteen, lingered as if he wanted to talk, then crouched in front of her with a reassuring grin.

"We're getting close now," he told her. "The Apaches were here two or three days ago but I don't think they've gone far. With prisoners they'd likely . . . ah . . . stop and camp to . . . ah . . . amuse themselves for a while. When we know where they are Wolf and I'll go after them and leave you with Lambert and Pop. He's not in any shape for a fight, but between them they can look after you. Just sit tight until we bring that map."

The smile she returned was a little tremulous. "Do you think you and Wolf alone can win against so many of them? Isn't that too dangerous for you?"

"I've seen longer odds before and I'm still here, and I mean to keep on being."

He left her then and walked to Garrison. They talked a little, the big, dark wolf looking somehow as sinister as his nickname in the gathering dark, the fair Loco a confident, easy-moving figure. As she spread her blanket Loco passed her to post himself on guard below their camp and the double watch was a comfort.

Until tonight they had used only one at a time, Loco, Wolf and Craig dividing the dark hours between them, but here it appeared they intended to go without any sleep. She had a pang of guilt and yet these two had about them the air of competence equal to any emergency.

Loco Smith sat in the dark shade of a rock where the moon would not make a target of him, his rifle in his lap, his blue eyes ranging restlessly and his ears tuned to the small sounds of night hunting animals. Any change in their pattern would warn him and his signal to Wolf would be a stone thrown up the trail toward him.

Alert by training that had grown into instinct, training that had kept him alive so long, the rest of his mind like a separate entity passed the time in daydreaming. He smiled, thinking about the sleeping girl, looking ahead to when her father's money would be found or lost and laying plans.

Lambert of course would be removed. That had been decided in Phoenix as soon as it was established that a man with the stamp of law officer would come with them. If Pop Engle lasted out the ordeal of the mountains he would have to be gotten rid of. That would narrow it down to himself and Wolf. The wolf required examination.

Loco knew he could outthink and outdraw the big partner but he must keep from being shot in the back himself. He would not object to dividing the hundred thousand dollars. It was Jerry Dillman he would not share, and from the way Garrison preened himself for her he was sure Wolf would put up an argument. They might cut cards for her but Loco did not like a game unless the odds were stacked heavily in his favor and the wolf would without doubt make sure they were not. There was the chance the wolf would win a cut. That left him the single choice.

Loco regretted that choice. He had found a kindred soul in Wolf Garrison and life was better with someone to ride with. Strange, the turns fate took a man on. If he had not ridden into Arizona to escape arrest in California he would not have played cards with the sheriff who liked aces. If he had not played cards he would not have shot the man. If he had not shot him he would not have gone to Yuma prison. If he had not landed there he might never have met the wolf. They would not have escaped in time to rescue Pop, nor come into the Superstitions for a treasure. They would not be on this mountain about to tackle an unknown number of Apache Indians, an unsatisfactory balance of odds. He would not have to sacrifice his partner.

But if the chain of events had broken anywhere he would never have met Jerry Dillman, and that meeting he classed as the single most important happening in his checkered life.

A fat orange moon lifted above the black jagged silhouette of the peaks and flooded the brutal land with soft light. It seemed to Loco Smith a promise that the days ahead would bring fulfillment for him. He smiled into the face of the moon, then looked away from it. It would not do to let the bright ball blind his night sight any longer. He might have need of it.

CHAPTER 10

In the morning Craig Lambert felt much better than he had expected to. The stone cuts on his face were scabbed over and the pain was gone. His head had quit throbbing and the gash only hurt when he touched it. The aloe had done its work well. It was his first acquaintance with the plant which did not grow in the colder climate of the northern states he was familiar with and he made a point of thanking Loco Smith for the doctoring. Aside from courtesy he did not want the antagonism that had flashed into the open the night before kept alive. He and Smith and Garrison were too interdependent at this stage. They could not afford to let the enmity between them distract them from a concentration on caution with the fact that there were Indians in the area. If Dillman's map still existed and was recoverable there had to be full co-operation among all of them.

They ate an early breakfast and he learned from Jerry's concerned questions about the double guard. Smith and Garrison had gone without sleep all the last day and the night and there was this day dawning. Without rest both men could be dull-witted when alertness might count most.

"I've done some tracking, used to trap," Craig said without adding that it was men like them he trailed. "If you can sleep in your saddles I can find the way."

Loco and the wolf exchanged looks that agreed they were sure he was an expert. The men Wells Fargo sent out to run down those they wanted brought in were like hounds. They were convinced the man before them was hunting Dillman's amassed fortune for that company and his being here was proof enough that he could follow a scent on the wind.

"We might as well use him." Loco was enigmatic. "Send him out ahead and I'll ride drag while you catch a nap, then we'll switch."

Lambert understood that one would stay awake to watch him but he said nothing in objection. The main thing was that they all keep as fresh as they could.

Pop Engle had to be helped into his saddle, the pack mules were tied on a lead rope behind him and the train set out. Jerry Dillman chose to ride at Lambert's side, which Garrison did not approve.

"I don't like it," he told Loco. "Her up there on scout with him. What if they find trouble?"

Loco chewed his lip and then shrugged. "I'd think he's got a nose for trouble if he is Wells Fargo and what else can he be? He was ready to chuck his job and let us ride away from him yesterday so he's going to take good care of her. Let it alone and let's get what good we can out of him as long as we can."

"I guess you're right," Garrison admitted and put his horse into line behind the pair, ahead of Gilbert Engle.

Craig Lambert did not take as far a lead as Garrison had. With Gilbert less than at his best and Garrison already sagging on his horse, asleep before they turned the bend, only the tired Loco Smith to watch the rear, he wanted the girl with him but close enough to send her back to the column if he sensed danger ahead.

He had no difficulty following the Indian trail. The moccasin prints might be faint but the shoes on the horses of the Albert party, three riding animals and two sets of the smaller hoofs of pack mules, churned the grit soil into a definite path. His rifle across his saddle, turning his head in continuous study of the land, he talked in low tones to Jerry Dillman. She had asked what more he knew about the Ghost Dancers, apparently caught in a fascination of horror.

"The Sioux and Cheyenne have adopted it most but many tribes are infected, even those in Oregon and now in Arizona."

She grimaced and pressed her inquiry. "Do you know who started it?"

"No one does exactly. In seventy-one a Nevada Paiute called Ta-vibo is presumed to have begun preaching the idea, claiming that the Great Spirit had appeared to him and told him the invaders who were destroying the buffalo and driving his chosen people away from their homes were going to be exterminated. He said a great earthquake would soon swallow all the people in America, red and white and he had an ingenious catch. Those Indians who purified themselves in the Ghost Dance would be resurrected and the country would belong to them again. There are various frills prophesied by other messengers but the final promise is the same."

"And the tribes believe fantasies like that? It sounds incredible."

"It isn't. If you were an Indian who had lost your hunting grounds, seen your women raped and murdered, the buffalo that furnished you ninety per cent of what you lived by slaughtered to force you onto reservations where you could barely exist, wouldn't you believe in something that offered a ray of hope?"

His vehemence made her wonder again about him and what his background was and she asked, "Where did you learn so much about it?"

86

He could not explain that he had helped set up stage routes, build stations to protect travelers, and he had wanted to know as much as he could learn about the people he was supposed to fight. In learning he had come to feel that the Indian was more sinned against than sinning and the fate they were facing was tragic.

"You get to know if you're around the West for long. What makes the Ghost Dance bad is that they work themselves up into frenzy and a mass-induced trance until they fall unconscious and when they come out of it they believe they have died and the Great Spirit has given them another life. Eternal life. They're not afraid to die again."

She sounded thoughtful with an undertone of fear in her tone. "It sounds like a frightful perversion of Christianity, Craig."

"It is, and the white man brought it on himself, preaching about a Prince of Peace on one hand and making war on the other at the same time. Can you wonder they're confused?" She did not answer and they rode on in silence, Jerry thinking about the compassion this big man had shown her, even in the face of Steve Albert's mutilated body.

Toward noon they found a surprise. A tiny trickle of clear water came out of the rock wall and slid down it into the trail, leaving hardly a trace of moisture. Lambert called a halt and the second Wolf Garrison's horse stopped the rider opened his eyes, fully awake.

Lambert got down, left the girl and walked a way farther ahead where he could listen, hear sounds that would be lost in the activity of the others. Garrison went immediately to the outfall and looked down on the darker ground under it, then toward Lambert and beyond him, his black eyes narrowed, nearly closed and his lean back teased. After a long moment he beckoned to Jerry and when she was at his side said quietly, "We're getting pretty close, kid. That was made late yesterday."

She looked down where he pointed, at a hoof print deep in the softer ground where the water fell, and half filled it. A little groan of apprehension escaped her.

The wolf grinned at her. "That's what we want, isn't it?"

He used the point of his thick-bladed hunting knife to gouge an undercut out of the wall so the trickle fell off it in free-flowing rapid drops, then handed his canteen to Jerry and grinned to quiet her nervousness.

"You want to take up a collection of these and reload them while I rustle some grub?"

She smiled back, glad of something to do except think about Apaches, and gathered the containers, holding one under the drip while she watched the men.

Loco Smith was dismounted and beside Pop Engle's horse, helping him down and steadying him, walking him to the spring. Pop sank wearily to the ground. Loco took the partly filled canteen from Jerry, handed it to Pop and when the old man had drunk two swallows took it back and dribbled what was left over the gray head and down the back of the neck, massaging it gently.

The water was cold, its source deep under the crest of the mountains, reviving Gilbert quickly.

Loco said, "Hang on, Pop, we've almost got that map in our hands." He pointed out the hoof print. "You'll be reading it pretty soon now."

Wolf Garrison caught his eye and jerked his head to bring Loco to him. "You read that track right?"

"I made it last evening. What do you think?"

"Uh-huh. I'm going to eat a bite, then go scout the trail so we don't all run into them unexpected. You get some sleep and wait here until I come back."

Loco debated. There was a good chance that the Apaches had already killed Ned Albert, left his body as they had Steve's and gone on. Ned must be carrying the map and if the wolf found it would he come back at all? Yes he would, Smith decided. With Jerry Dillman here the treasure would not be enough to make him leave her to find it alone. Furthermore the Indians might find Garrison and that would remove his major problem.

"Go to it," he said, and went off to rig the blanket shelters.

He had crawled under one and was asleep by the time Wolf Garrison told Craig Lambert where he was going and why and rode out.

Within two miles the wolf's instinct warned him the Indians were near. He climbed a low ridge, got off the horse beneath the top and crawled on to survey the trail beyond. There was another canyon, then another ridge and although he lay there a long time nothing moved except a deer in the bottom. That told him there were no Apaches short of the far crest.

He mounted and rode down, then up and again crept to look ahead. This time the picture was different. Instead of a canyon he looked into a round bowl enclosed by jagged peaks. And in the bowl brown figures, moved around a curl of rising smoke. They were out of rifle range and with the treachery of the shades and brush down there he could not count them or tell what they were doing. And both were important pieces of information to report back.

He tied the horse and crawled over the ridge toward the narrow mouth of the valley, his knife between his teeth, watchful for a sentry that he expected to be guarding the pass. He found none, then he was through and in among the rock upthrusts that studied the slopes from the top of the peaks to the valley floor.

He moved from one of these to another, as wily as an Apache himself, not directly down but circling at an angle toward a shoulder that jutted into the bowl just above the fire. From that he could have a close look even in the failing light.

His caution cost time. The shadow was deep before he reached the shoulder and he took advantage of every shade to slip out to the nose. The Indians were out of his sight until he arrived at that end and when he could see them again he made discoveries that drew his mouth to a straight, tight line.

As darkness thickened the fire had been built up. Its red glow brightened the dark skins of not six or seven but twelve Apaches. Naked except for breechclouts they danced around a stake where a naked white man was tied. The prisoner's head hung forward as if he were unconscious, which Garrison imagined he was glad to be, but he must not have been so for long. One Indian broke the stamping circle, went to the stake, yanked the head up by its hair, shook it, then dropped it and walked to the other side of the fire. The dancers stopped and moved to join him.

Garrison said under his breath, "No fun badgering a man when he don't know it, I guess."

The Apaches had another game now, taking up lances and one after another running and throwing them at a target close to the ground, a head. The wolf thought it had been cut off the second prisoner until the third lance drove into the ground inches from it and the head jerked away. It was still attached to a live man buried up to his chin.

These were valuable pieces of information. Both Ned Albert and No Shoes Johnson were alive as of the moment. How long they would stay alive Garrison could not guess, but it was time to clear out of here, get back to the camp and bring in the troops.

He had begun the retreat but stopped in mid step. One Apache was running toward the shoulder where he crouched. Wolf had left his rifle with the horse and had only his knife and short gun. If only one Indian had discovered him the knife would be enough. If more of them came at him he could stand them off for a while but the odds of killing all of them before they swarmed over him were too long for comfort.

Then the running figure veered along the path, which Garrison now saw skirted the edge of the bowl, and headed up toward the pass just under the ridge. He would be the sentry the wolf had not found on his way in, either coaxed away from his post to the pleasure of joining the dancing and jousting, discovered by the leader of the band and ordered back or been down for something to eat. Perhaps they did not keep a constant watch. They had obviously felt secure on their way here, not taking the least trouble to cover the marks of their passage, so they might be satisfied with only a periodic inspection.

Garrison was not interested in reasons. He was interested in that figure on its way to block his exit from this valley. If it went only as far as the mouth and waited there that would not be too bad, but if it crossed the ridge and found the horse Wolf was in trouble. A hue and cry would be raised, the pass bottled up tight and when daylight came the bunch of them would dig him out. The wolf did not enjoy the prospect.

It would take too long to go around the way he had come to the shoulder. The Indian could be yelling his warning before he got half way. The firelight did not hit this side of the shoulder and at the bottom of it the path was beyond the circle of glow. There would be moonlight later but the trail was dark now. Using it was a risk but he did not see a choice.

Hurrying, he still took care, shoved his gun under his belt where it would not swing loose in the holster and perhaps strike a rock with sharp sound and tested every step before he put his weight on it.

The sentry was swallowed by the night when Garrison came off the slope. He had a thought that shocked him. The Apache might only be out here to relieve himself, might be very close in front of him. He flared his nostrils and breathed deeply but all his nose identified was smoke.

He prowled up the path with his knife in his hand, not looking forward to fighting the Indian with it. The Apaches were noted as the finest knife men on the long frontier.

A drum began a rapid rhythm back by the fire. That was no help. It could dull some sound Wolf Garrison needed to hear. He went up the path with long, swift, silent strides, all his senses straining. As he approached the pass the sky, lightened a little by far-off stars, showed him the open mouth and the dark walls framing it. There was no Indian standing against the light but he could be against the black hulk of the hill.

Garrison stopped after every step now to listen and to test the air. He had the one advantage that he knew the man was somewhere in the vicinity while the Apache did not yet know Wolf was here. There would be plenty of noise if he found out.

The wolf held his knife point up against his thigh, stepped into the gap holding his breath, then moved through it up toward the ridge keeping close against the wall. The darkness there hid him and he could not be attacked from that side. The rock was still hot to the touch but the breeze on Garrison's wet face felt cold.

Under his feet the slant of the ground changed, leveled off for the crest and then dropped down. Wolf was only a hundred feet from where he had tied the horse. He moved on, pantherlike through the growing glow of the moon that would soon rise.

Then the smell was in his nose, of rancid grease in lank hair and rank body odor.

Wolf stopped, peering into the gloom, not knowing whether the savage was before him, behind or on one side. A surprised grunt gave him a direction and Garrison swung that way, sure he was discovered and not able to see the enemy.

While he stood poised for an attack the moon edged up over the high mountain and in the first faint light Wolf had a picture, the Indian standing beside the horse. The surprise had been at finding the animal. The Apache turned from it, looking for the rider, and located Garrison easing toward him twenty feet away.

The Apache's knife caught a flash of moonlight as he drew it and Garrison saw the mouth open wide to yell, then Wolf had jumped, his knife thrust out before him and the yell cut off without sound.

92

The Indian's empty hand clamped on Garrison's wrist and he drove his blade toward the wolf's armpit. Garrison grabbed the arm and snapped it down. He was bigger, stronger than the Indian but the sinewy fingers were like a vice, keeping Wolf's blade from reaching the brown body.

The Indian flung out a leg, trying to get the moccasined heel behind Garrison's knee and dump him but Wolf yanked him off balance. The Apache found his footing in a quick jump and they swayed like dancers with both knife hands deadlocked.

Garrison's superior weight won out. He hauled the Indian in against him, then threw him away. The brown body stumbled back, one foot tripped and the man fell, Garrison dropping on top of him, knocking the wind out of the slighter Apache.

He lay stunned for a second and Garrison used the time to twist his wrist and force his blade down toward the corded throat. The man beneath him dropped his knife and Wolf's wrist and used both hands to wrestle the arm away, squirming, wriggling free, rolling toward the knife on the ground.

Garrison stabbed him in the side, again in the throat, saw the gush of blood as the Apache died. He crawled five feet away and lay flat on his back, filling his lungs in heaving pants until he regained the strength to get up.

He cleaned his knife in the hard earth, found the gun that had fallen out of his belt and picked up the Apache's knife. The moon was well above the mountain now, giving him light to see the dead man clearly. The Indian was less than five foot five with an old, starved face as though he had never had enough to eat.

Wolf Garrison did not like touching him again but he could not leave him here. When the Indians in the valley missed him they would look for him and finding him would forewarn them. He took the rope off his saddle horn, slung the body over the rump of the horse and tied it there. The horse shied at the blood smell. Garrison slapped the rein across its nose and kept a tight hold while he scraped the dirt the fight had kicked loose over the blood on the ground.

Then he mounted and rode toward the camp. It was a mile before he found what he was looking for, a split in the edge of the trail where rock had broken away and he could go close enough to the lip without danger. There he untied the body, let it slide and toed it over the drop.

Coming close to the camp he called ahead. He did not want to be mistaken and shot. Loco's voice answered from a perch above and Smith scrambled down.

"You find them?"

"Uh-huh."

"Is Albert still alive?"

"I don't know." Wolf spoke in a low voice that the girl could not hear, telling about the man at the stake and the one buried to his neck. "I don't know which is which and neither one looked in much shape. They may be dead by now."

"How many Apaches?"

"I counted eleven, plus one I knifed."

Loco Smith's eyes widened. "There weren't that many in the bunch we've been following. The rest must have stayed at their camp. You got any idea how we get Albert away from them?"

Garrison grinned. "You could pull your Great Spirit stunt again."

"Not with broncos, they're too sharp."

"I guess. But what I figure, they're going to celebrate all night or until they fall down, and if we start now we can be at that valley by daylight. They're going to be pretty worn out for a fight and if we're lucky we may catch most of them asleep. We can all go together as far as where I staked out my horse on this side of the rim, then you and Lambert and I can work on in to the shoulder I watched from. Ought to be like shooting fish in a barrel."

Loco said emphatically, "Oh no, we don't take Lambert. I don't want a lawman with a gun in his hand close to me. I could just accidentally get shot. If the setup is like you say we can do it alone."

The wolf looked startled and said slowly, "I didn't think of that. Yeah, I'm with you . . . well, let's get started."

CHAPTER 11

They waked the sleeping girl, Lambert and Gilbert Engle.
Loco wanted to leave Pop with the pack animals but the old
man would have none of it. Without his saying so it was plain
he did not trust Loco or Garrison to come back if they got the
map and he swore he would follow them on his own if they left
him behind. Loco was sure that if he did leave the mules un-
tended some hunting cat would make a meal of them, so the
whole party lined out in Garrison's wake.

Jerry Dillman rode as close as possible to Craig Lambert, her
knee brushing his and her heart pounding. Now that she herself had seen the savagery of the Indians she had scoffed at she
wished desperately that she had not insisted on coming here,
but it was much too late to change that now. All she could do
was trust these men, who indeed had been equal to every con-
tingency that had risen so far. The ride was eerie to her, with
the moonlight making grotesque shapes of the rocky spires and

tumbled masses, creating a foreign world unrelentingly forbidding.

Where the wolf had left his horse earlier the trail widened in a draw with room for all the animals. It was now near dawn and Wolf hurried his instuctions to Lambert.

"Loco and I are going in, and you stay here to look after Jerry." Seeing the doubt and revolt in Lambert's outthrust jaw, knowing that Lambert had no more faith in their returning than Gilbert did, he added solemnly, "Mister, you can count on this, I'm not going anywhere unless this girl goes with me and I'm sure not taking her along now. Just rest easy and stay put."

Lambert resented taking any order from these outlaws but Jerry Dillman's safety was more important to him than anything and he gave Garrison a curt nod and turned his back, feeling secure from a back shot while the girl was in his trust.

Loco Smith had pulled his and Garrison's rifles from the boots and as the wolf started for the ridge tossed his to him and trailed quietly behind him. They were stealthy going into the pass because the Apaches could have learned their sentry was gone and posted another, but no one jumped them.

The fire still burned, winking when the dark figures crossed in front of it. Garrison was less careful this time in leading Loco to the shoulder and they were on the point before the morning moon paled and first light touched the higher ground.

It was still dark on the valley floor but the firelight showed them the dancers, still shuffling around it, drunk with exhaustion, reeling. There were only six still on their feet and these now wore the buffalo hide and horn masks of a ritual. Garrison whispered that it must be the Ghost Dance which very few white men had witnessed and lived to describe.

He crouched with Loco waiting for light enough below to show them where the missing Indians were, and as it grew the remaining dancers dropped out one by one. The last one stumbled to a stop and sank down with his head falling between his legs. The wolf nudged Loco and they raised their rifles, each choosing one side of the dying fire, pouring bullets into the bowl.

In a deathlike trance they might have been but the Apaches came out of it at the first blast. Generations of being surrounded by danger had instilled in them an instinct for survival that transcended the utmost weariness. They rolled to their feet, transfixed for a moment, pivoting to find the source of the attack.

The first two targets did not move and two more fell during the short Indian orientation, then they were running, scattering toward the surrounding rocky walls. Two snatched up guns and ammunition belts from a stack of arms. Loco shot one but the other dived into the safety of the lower boulders. The rest had been exceedingly quick in finding cover. Six Apaches escaped, all presumably wearing their knives and one carrying a rifle, scrambling through the rocks that edged the trail out of the valley.

Both Garrison and Loco concentrated on that one, firing whenever they caught a glimpse of dark skin dodging from one shelter to another, but the opportunities were too fleeting and the Indian was not moving in a predictable line. They could not tell where to expect him next although he was apparently making for the pass.

"We're just wasting lead," Loco decided. "Hold it and let's get down there. Lambert will pick him off when he goes through the gap."

The nose of the shoulder was steep and they went down it in jumping steps, their attention divided between where their feet would land and watching for the Apache's movement. It was now light enough to make out the Albert party's horses and mules staked in a bunch, the saddles thrown aside and the packs opened and raided, gear the Indians had no use for discarded.

Wolf Garrison said anxiously, "I hope that map wasn't in those saddlebags. If it was it's sure gone now."

He did not go looking for it at once, angling to the cache of guns. The Albert arms were the newest there and the others a sorry collection. Three were Mexican guns, French made and brought over by Maximilian's soldiers when the Austrian had Napoleon's help in trying to make himself Emperor of Mexico. The wolf stood his rifle against a rock and methodically broke the others so no Indian might slip down again and be able to use them.

Loco headed for the closest prisoner, the one tied at the stake, put his ear against the chest and sighed in relief when he heard the heartbeat. It was even encouragingly strong. He cut the man free and eased him to the ground, then ran to the one buried, not knowing which was Ned Albert.

The buried one was dead with a lance through one eye, a grisly, bloody head that flies crawled over, making it look as if the mouth was working. Loco grimaced and started back for the living man and as he turned the Apache on the hillside started shooting.

Loco and Wolf jumped for cover but it was not them the Indian was aiming at. A horse fell, then another, as the rifle was used to put the men afoot. The spurts of gunsmoke came from behind a cluster of rocks near the top of the rise and the Indian was out of sight behind them.

Loco shrugged. "We're out of his range, Wolf. Just keep him pinned there and let him whang away while I see who this guy is."

There were four Indian shelters, hides stretched between rocks to make shade, and under the closest one Loco found a skin of water, took it to the limp man on the ground and dribbled it into the open mouth and onto the face that was pale under its sunburn. He slapped the cheeks gently and after a time the chest heaved in a deep breath and the man opened his eyes. There was pain and terror in them that only gradually changed as he saw a white man bending over him.

Loco Smith said, "You Ned Albert, I hope?"

There was a weak nod. Loco called to Wolf, "We've got Albert," and lifted the head to give more water, to keep the man from losing consciousness again. "You'll be all right now," he encouraged. "The Indians are gone. Can you talk?"

Albert tried but no sound came. Loco sat him up, leaned him against his shoulder so he could drink without strangling and fed water to him sparingly until the first whispered words sighed out of the throat.

"Thanks. I was about gone. Who are you?"

"Friends of yours. We've been looking for you. Came to help you find that money. You still got the map, haven't you?"

Ned Albert groaned. It sounded as though he believed he might as well not have been rescued from the Apaches, that he was in no kinder hands now. Loco confirmed it, chuckling.

"I hope for your sake you do, Ned, because without it you don't stand much chance of getting away from here."

Albert groaned again and whispered, "Either way you'll let me die. I've got no chance anyhow."

"No we won't. If you have it we'll help get your strength back and then go looking together."

A rasping laugh shook Albert and he said, "Sure we will, but it won't do you any good if I give it to you. We looked everywhere and never saw anything like it describes. It's a fake. That Dillman only wanted to get his partner killed, sending him in here."

"Then you shouldn't mind showing it to us. Where is it?"

Albert surrendered as the only slim alternative he had to stay alive. "Sewed in the tail of my shirt, whatever those devils did with it."

"Fine."

Loco moved Albert, propped him against a rock and put the water skin in his hands and stood up to look around the camp. A bullet whistled too close. Loco dropped flat against the ground, looking toward Wolf Garrison and yanking his side gun. He thought the wolf had overheard Albert and now was trying to kill him, but Garrison was still facing the hill, firing that way, spacing his shots. The wolf, too, was keeping down behind a boulder and Loco watched where he was aiming. It was lower than where the Indian had been earlier. The animals were all dead and the Apache had worked down to put the men within his range.

Loco reached for his rifle and began firing at the side of the rock opposite the one Wolf was peppering and the Indian dodged higher. With that Loco went in search of Ned Albert's shirt. There were no clothes near the scatter of the pack bags, none near the stake or anywhere else in sight. He headed for the hide shelters, found a coat in the first one and the shirt in the second, filched by an Apache. Squatting in the shade he examined the shirttail and located a patch sewed near the bottom. He was pulling his knife to cut it open when a new voice yelled from a distance.

"I got him."

Loco put his head out and saw Craig Lambert standing at the valley edge of the gap, lowering his rifle.

Loco Smith dropped the shirt, forgot about maps and hidden treasures as in his mind he saw Jerry Dillman left with only Pop Engle to protect her and five live Apaches loose on the mountain between himself and the blond girl.

He yelled and ran. Wolf Garrison was already running. The horror was that Craig Lambert, too, was running. Down the path toward them. Behind him Loco barely heard Ned Albert's cry for them not to leave him.

Garrison paused and swung his rifle up toward Lambert and Loco shouted to stop him from shooting the lawman.

"Wolf. . . . Not now. . . . May need him bad . . ."

The wolf heard, lowered the gun and ran on. He and Lambert met more than halfway down the hill and Garrison's balled fist lashed out, hit Lambert's chin and knocked him flat. The wolf did not pause to see him fall but raced toward the top as fast as his legs would pump.

Lambert had just got his feet under him again when Loco reached him, swung from his shoulder and knocked him down again, jumped over him and rushed on after Wolf.

Lambert scrambled up the second time, shaking his head. His first thought was that these two had found the map and were racing to be on their way, but there was something so desperate in their frantic climb that a chill fear shot through him and he raced after them.

CHAPTER 12

Craig Lambert ran through the pass and looked down on the place a hundred feet below where he had left Jerry Dillman and Pop Engle. Engle was there, sprawled on the ground. Loco and Wolf were there, frozen, looking up the side draw. The pack mules were there. The saddles were there. All of the horses were gone. And so was Jerry Dillman.

A high cry wrenched from Lambert. "Where is she?"

He jumped down the grade, his eyes searching among the rocks. Garrison swung toward him, raging, shouting.

"You left her. You let them get her. Why the . . ."

Lambert felt the blood run out of him, leave him cold. "The shooting. . . . There was so much I thought you were in trouble. I went to see. I saw six dead Indians and killed another one. That's all there were. Isn't it?" His voice shook, out of control.

Loco Smith said bleakly, "There were eleven, Lambert. Five

got clear. They don't have guns but they do have knives. They have Jerry Dillman."

"I wasn't gone ten minutes. Maybe the shooting frightened her and she hid. . . ." But by the hollowness of his tone he knew that was not so.

Garrison cursed him. "She put a knife in Gilbert's back? She took the horses somewhere?"

Loco Smith glanced at the pack mules, but the little beasts would throw anyone who tried to ride them. He unlashed the packs, dropped them, filled his pockets with jerky, slung a canteen over his shoulder and walked into the side draw, where the hoof prints were plain. He knew he could not overtake the horses on foot but it was something to do, something to focus his mind on. He wiped it clear of all pictures of the blond girl as Apache captive.

Wolf Garrison followed Loco's lead in taking provisions, then went after him. Craig Lambert went last, some distance behind them, numbed and bitter against himself, equally bitter against these men. Why had they not told him there were more Indians? Garrison must have found it out on his scouting sortie and he should have been warned. Because they had no high opinion of him they, too, were responsible for the girl's capture. But the main guilt was his to live with.

Loco and Garrison talked in low voices about where the Indians might go. The trail continued rising. Would it take them over the range and down the far side or to some higher campsite?

By sunset they had walked nearly ten miles and gradually they became aware that they were circling in a long swing around the gaunt ridges. The Indians were no longer climbing, nor were they heading out of the hills. Darkness forced a halt and the three men sagged down to the ground. None of them wanted to stop but they could not see the tracks without light. The moon would help later but the waiting for it would be an agony.

Loco Smith said out of the long silence, "They're not in a hurry and they haven't stopped anywhere this far. I think I know what they're doing. They're trying to wear us down until we can't track them any longer. Then they'll go home."

Craig Lambert said, "Where do you mean, home?"

"Back to that bowl. Wolf, you know Apaches, wouldn't you say that was a headquarters camp that they use when they're in this area? Those hides stretched for shelters have been there awhile, been wet and shrunk taut."

"That's so." The wolf's voice sharpened. "And there's something else I should have thought of before, but losing that girl made my head stop working. They left ovens full of bread cooking, a lot of it, enough to feed them for days. They're not going off and leave that behind."

"Bread?" Lambert said. "Where would they get any meal to make it with?"

"They don't use meal. They know how to live off the desert plants, cactus for instance. They dig a little pit and put hot stones in the bottom, then they spread the pulp of the agave over them and cover it for twenty-four hours. That makes mescal, they use it like bread."

"Mescal is a liquor like pulque, I thought," Loco argued.

"It's both. For the drink they cook the pulp a lot longer, then soak it and ferment it in the sun. . . . We're wasting time here." The wolf stood up. "I don't know about you but I'm going back to that valley and wait for them."

"Now? In the dark? You'll get lost," Lambert objected.

"I don't get lost, mister. I could find my way back there blind by feeling the rocks. I memorized every one at every turn, in every canyon. You going with me or staying here? You stay and you'll never see that blonde again."

Loco got to his feet and after a hesitation Lambert followed, not convinced that he would ever see her anyway, but it was at least possible that the outlaw was right and he could not follow the trail endlessly. They started back the way they had come, able to see only the shadowy shapes of each other in the faint starlight. Wolf Garrison had made a discovery.

Talking helped him keep from thinking about the girl and he said, "We'll have a surprise for them. They know we have guns and all they have is Pop's rifle and short arm. They know we're on foot too and they'll figure that if they lead us around these hills long enough to run out of water and wear our boots off we'll give up and try to make it outside, or die. It's an old Apache trick, Victorio used it against Major Morrow near Ojo Caliente, baited the troops to trail him until he wore them down and then slipped over the border to Mexico."

Craig Lambert, too, found a temporary solace in voices and purely to keep Wolf going he said, "How do you know what Victorio did?"

"I was there," the wolf lied, and because he suspected Lambert came from the San Francisco Bay area where Wells Fargo headquartered and had seen how unfamiliar he was with the Southwest he took the opportunity of reading him a lecture. He knew it would gall the lawman and at the moment it was the only way he could think of to take a revenge on him. "When you ride into a country you don't know you'd better believe the people who live there know some things you don't. The reason Arizona is so full of burned-out cabins and abandoned ranches is because the Johnny-come-latelys never get through their heads that in spite of the forts and the soldiers the Apaches control ninety per cent of the territory and they just do not like white men. You mean to stay hereabouts you'd better listen."

Lambert choked down his temper, asking, "Then I suppose you can tell me why if that valley is as permanent a camp as you say there were no women or children."

"Because it's a bronco camp. They're bucks who broke off the reservation and threw off the tribal authority. Every hand is against them, their own people would fight them if they could find them. They'll steal a woman and use her and leave her dead or alive but wishing she wasn't, but they move too fast to be bothered with anybody who'd slow them down."

"Where did you learn so much about Indians?"

Wolf Garrison almost licked his lips at this chance to haze the tenderfoot agent. "I don't usually advertise this," he said solemnly, "but I lived with the 'Paches for a year. I'd run away from home and joined a wagon train going West. We got as far as Apache Pass, then Mangas Coloradas and his Mimbrenos hit us. They killed everybody but me. . . ."

Loco Smith's head snapped up and he blinked in the dark. Mangas Coloradas, Red Sleeves, had surrendered to the army and been murdered in 1863. That would make Wolf Garrison close to five years old at the time he said the wagon train was massacred. Loco had a wry grin at the picture of a boy that age running away from home, and he listened in admiration as the tale spun on.

"I hid under a wagon until it was over, then I crawled out. There was a Mexican woman, one of Mangus's wives, who knew some English. Being as dark as I am I told her I was the son of an Apache woman who my father stole from the reservation. I said he'd deserted her and took me back East with him but he beat me so much I ran off to find my mother's people."

"And she believed you?" Loco chuckled.

"I'm here, aren't I?" The wolf's voice was all innocence.

"So they adopted you? How come you left them?"

"Why, the band was rounded up by soldiers and we were all sent to San Carlos agency. I'd made myself solid with Mangas by then, saved one of his daughters' lives . . . the one who married Cochise, and I was getting along fine but everybody hated that agency. The agent had a game, he'd lean a ladder against a wall and throw the rations we were supposed to get at it. Whatever stuck on the rungs we got, and everything that went through he sold to the Tucson Ring. So I ducked out and went to Tucson where the food was."

Craig Lambert was more than a little suspicious of Garrison's adventures and that took him the next step, back to a doubt that the wolf really thought the Indians would return to the camp in the bowl. His grim thought was that more likely the outlaw's apparent fascination for Jerry Dillman was only as deep as Apache lust. With his black hair and eyes he might indeed have Apache blood. The chilling idea took hold that Garrison had given up on finding her and now wanted only to save his own neck, was leading them back to the trail with the intention of slipping off, abandoning her and the elusive money both. He stopped abruptly and drew his short gun, raising his voice.

"You're both covered. Now listen to me. I don't believe one word you've said since you turned us back. All you mean to do is get away from these mountains, Garrison, and I am putting a stop to your tricks. You turn yourselves around, both of you, and follow that girl."

Loco Smith turned carefully with no quick move, saying across his shoulder, "Seems like you overdid it, Wolf. Lambert, you've got a right not to believe some of that whopper but the part about circling to the valley makes good sense. It's true that Colorado pulled the same stunt on the army. Besides, it's the only possibility we have of finding her now."

Lambert was long in reacting. So much time had passed that Jerry could already be dead. There seemed little likelihood that they might find her unharmed.

Loco Smith gave him time to figure that out, then added his clincher. "We'd better move if we're going to get there before they do and we can't save her if they see us first."

"All right then." Lambert's voice came through clenched teeth. "But if they don't come there I'll kill you both."

The wolf shrugged and started walking again, unhappily aware that the lawman followed them with his gun still in his hand.

The moon came up when they were halfway to the trail and they made better time. When they came close to it a slither of movement made Loco and Garrison draw quickly, then they saw the gaunt form of a mountain cat bound away from the carcasses of the pack mules. Pop Engle's body was gone, dragged off into the rocks by some animal to be eaten in solitude.

Now that they had guns in their hands too, Loco and Wolf felt more comfortable, but that did not last long. The wolf stopped them just short of the trail with a warning.

"From here on we don't leave footprints. They'll be looking for sign and I don't want to advertise we're here."

As an example he took off his shirt, dropped it and took off his boots, tied the laces together and slung them around his neck, then shoved his rifle under his belt against his back so it would not drag along the ground. He put his hands down the sleeves of the shirt but balled the cuffs into a cushion for his fists and twisted the body of the shirt into a loose cord. He got down on his knees and began crawling, off to the side of the trail, circling around the rocks in his way.

Loco and Lambert did the same and they crept up to the pass and through it, staying on the rubble against the wall. In the valley moonlight made black shadows that ran out from the tumbled rock and threw a soft glow over everything else.

Nothing moved below them. The Apaches could already be here but if they were they had made no fire and had hidden the live horses. The dead animals were bloated mounds already torn apart by predators. It took intent searching to pick out the bodies of the Indians who had been killed here and when he located those Wolf was almost certain the others had not yet returned. Indians buried their dead quickly in the desert hot country. It could be a trap that they were left lying where they had fallen but he did not believe it. The circling horsemen knew they were too far ahead of those following on foot to have set an ambush this soon even supposing they thought the white men could walk behind them this far.

"Let's go down and stake it out," he said. "We want to be out of this light as soon as we can."

Garrison kept the lead down the trail to the floor. Not until they reached the bottom did they stand up, dress and walk along the path to the foot of the shoulder. Loco Smith angled away to the shelter where he had dropped the shirt. It was not where he thought it should be and he struck a match. There was no shirt there. He was still making certain when a scrambling noise in the rocks outside brought him out, his rifle leveled. He had a sidelong glimpse of Garrison and Lambert tensed and watchful, then Ned Albert called.

"God, am I glad it's you. I heard you coming and thought the Indians were back."

He came out of his hiding place, staggering with the weakness that he had not thrown off and Loco was relieved that the man was dressed, wearing the important shirt.

"They will be." Garrison sounded sure. "Any time from now on. You strong enough to handle a gun?"

Albert reached for the short arm the wolf held toward him but Loco knocked the hand away.

"Later. First, Lambert, you get up on that shoulder and keep watch . . . and don't go to sleep. If you see or hear them toss a stone down but don't fire until Wolf and I do or you'll warn them too soon."

Craig Lambert fumed at eating this crow, but until he knew Jerry Dillman's fate he would take any insult these outlaws threw at him. Without answering he began climbing the steep bank.

When the lawman's back was turned Loco caught Albert's arm and swung him toward the shelter. Under the hide roof he shoved him away.

"Take it off, Albert."

"I need it. It's cold up this high."

Loco raised his rifle as Wolf Garrison stepped in behind them, curious. Ned Albert looked from one to the other, then peeled off the shirt and tossed it at Loco.

"Keep him covered, Wolf," Loco said.

He laid aside his long gun, went out to the dead fire, gathered a handful of charred wood and half-burned bits and took them back inside the shelter. There he blew up a little flame and in its light picked up the shirt and with his knife point slit the patch open. When he picked out the folded paper Garrison made a low growl of pleasure.

They had their first look at Dilly Dillman's map. It was stained with sweat but it looked explicit enough. There were no measurements of distances, though the impression was left that the X in a circle was far closer to Broken Ax Canyon than the place where the Alberts had been captured. The directions were not, after all, in code. Loco read aloud.

Find the rock that looks like a horse head. Go to it and turn west into the draw under it for twenty-five steps. There is a cave hollowed out by wind. Dig away the rubble that looks like a natural rockslide. The money box is buried there.

The familiar prickling thrill tingled through Loco Smith. It always came when he felt close to a big win at cards or any other gamble, this pre-taste of money soon to be his.

The wolf took the map and studied it, trying to orient its indicated canyons and peaks and visualize the ground they had covered in relation to the drawing. Ned Albert put Wolf's thoughts into words.

"We looked at every rock for miles and there isn't one like any horse's head. I tell you, Dillman just wanted to get Gilbert killed."

CHAPTER 13

Jerry Dillman, raised as a city girl and longing for a wider knowledge of the world for the excitement of travel and adventure, had never included terror in her dreams. Now it was a cloud around her so dense she could not see through it.

She had had no slightest warning that anyone was closer than the men in the valley. She had heard their shooting, so much of it that Craig Lambert had looked worried and finally told Pop Engle to take care of her while he went to see if Loco and Wolf needed help. He had barely disappeared through the pass when five almost naked brown men with fierce black eyes and black hair in strings around their shoulders had materialized out of thin air.

Old Pop Engle had not been able to fire a shot. The first movement she had seen was an Indian landing on his back and driving a long knife hilt deep through his neck. He had fallen in a heap with blood welling out of the cut and his mouth and nose.

Jerry was too shocked to even think of trying to get away. She did not resist when her wrist was grabbed by dark fingers as strong as steel, but stood staring into the evil face that glared back at her without expression.

She was spun around so that her wrist was behind her, then the other wrist was pulled back against it and a thong tied them together and was brought up, wrapped around her neck and tied. She could not move her arms without choking herself. Next the Apache tied a lariat around her waist. The smell of him so close to her was so strong it sickened her.

Vaguely she was aware that the four others slashed the girths and shoved the saddles off the horses and swung up bareback and rode off up the draw. Her captor was last to mount. He jerked his head at her and kicked the horse into a walk. She had to follow at a half run or be pulled down and dragged.

Within half a mile she was gasping, a red haze wheeling behind her eyes, but she kept her feet for another hundred feet before she fell. She landed face down in the sharp grit and pain brought water to her eyes. She tasted blood on her mouth and her body heaved for breath.

She saw feet in moccasins step close to her head, heard a voice say something in a language she did not understand. She lay breathing heavily but a moment later she was grabbed by her hair and yanked up again.

The Indian said something else, some order, went back to the horse and rode on, though not as fast. The lariat pulled taut and she stumbled ahead but lasted only a hundred feet. Staggering, she fell again, all but unconscious. She began to cry aloud.

The Indian came back a second time, rolled her on her back with his foot and scowled down on her so ferociously that she caught her breath, expecting him to run his long knife into her.

He did bend down, but to pick her up, carry her to the horse and throw her across it. He mounted behind her and jogged on to catch up with his party, holding a handful of her dress to keep her from jouncing off. The blood running into her head filled it to bursting, then mercifully she blacked out.

When she came to she was on the ground again with the Apaches sitting cross-legged in a circle around her, talking among themselves. They saw that she was awake and got up at once. Her captor jumped to the back of the horse and another lifted her, passed her up to him and flung one of her legs over the animal. They rode now with one sinewy arm holding her against him. She did not know what to look forward to but at least she was not being run to death. Too weak to sit straight she sagged against the Indian, let her head fall against his hard shoulder and shut her eyes.

They rode for hours. The sun climbed, passed the zenith and began to sink, but she was too dazed to know which way they were going. They stopped once, cut the head off a barrel cactus and chewed the juicy pulp, shoving a piece into her mouth, then were on their way again.

A rattler buzzed and the man at the front of the column threw a knife at it, pinned the ugly head against the ground and got down, slung the thick body around his neck, mounted and went on.

An hour before dark they stopped in a canyon bottom. Jerry Dillman was lifted off the horse and set against a boulder, the lariat tied around it. A little fire was built. The snake was skinned out, cut into pieces and cooked, each man turning a stick skewered through a length over the flame. A smoking section was brought to her but her stomach revolted and she turned her head away. The Apache slapped her hard, wound his fingers in her hair, forced her mouth open and shoved the meat in. It burned her bruised lips but looking at that vicious face she was afraid of what the man would do if she did not obey so she sank her teeth into the snake, chewed and swallowed. Terrified as she was she tasted nothing.

They ignored her after that. The lariat around the boulder

was loose enough that she could lie down and the thong binding her wrists did not cut off circulation, but the only partially comfortable position she could find was on her stomach. Exhausted, she slept the night that way.

They roused her shortly after daybreak. Again she was put in the saddle with the Indian holding her. Twisting up and down canyons where she could see no trail she began wondering if the Indians were lost. She was almost afraid to wonder why men as savage as these had not molested her. While she had grown up convinced that the stories of Indian atrocity were like most of the other reports written by the flamboyant, overimaginative editors of the papers, the experiences of the last two days had reversed her ideas and she waited helplessly for the worst to be visited on her. But the iron arm around her waist was as indifferent to her body as if it were really metal.

They rested once during the blazing day where there was water, put their captive in the shade of a ragged spire and sought shade of their own, stretching on the ground for a siesta. The heat had kept Jerry drowsy, swaying on the horse and she lay down gratefully to sleep.

She did not know how long she had been there when she was startled awake. Someone was cutting the thong that bound her wrists. For a flashing moment she thought it was Craig Lambert, that somehow the men had found her, had slipped up on the sleeping Indians, then the hope was dashed and new horror sprang in its place. She was rolled onto her back and an Apache with a knife scar that drew his mouth into a leer was kneeling over her, his hands pinning her shoulders to the ground. She screamed.

He clamped one palm across her mouth but too late. The other Indians came rolling up, her captor running toward her, pulling his knife and yelling. The scar-faced man jumped back, rattling Apache words with the inflection of a question and pointing an open hand down at her. The other shook his head, flung one arm in the direction they had been riding and gave some harsh order.

Jerry sat up, cringing away and rubbing at her wrists as an argument developed between the two, then they were appealing to the three who had gathered around them, laughing. Her captor stood his ground, not laughing, talking urgently not so much as though he were claiming her for himself alone as that he insisted they take her someplace else before any of them used her.

Her captor won out and she had a reprieve for however long, but that scarcely helped and her heart sank. The one ray of hope returned, the thought that Lambert and Loco and Wolf could be following, but on foot she knew there was little possibility of their reaching her in time.

The siesta was spoiled, her wrists were tied anew, she was mounted in front of the Indian and the ride continued. Not far ahead they came to a place she recognized, where the mules lay, but Pop Engle's body was no longer in sight. They turned toward the valley. Then she knew two things.

The Indians had made a wide circle expecting to be followed, putting a long distance between themselves and the men who must walk, intending that the white men would exhaust themselves and die of thirst in the parched mountains. They would not be aware that Wolf Garrison knew the secrets of the desert hills. Her last resort of hope lay in Craig Lambert. He knew much about Indians. Did he know enough to predict that they would bring her back here? If he did not she was doomed. It was to that valley her captor had insisted she be taken. In that valley she was to be raped.

The stories came back to her of white women held captive by these people, even of some who when they were found chose to stay with their Indian mates and children, but she could never stay with this band. If they did not kill her she must find a way to kill herself.

As the Apaches climbed the last two ridges they studied the

ground of the trail. The last prints they saw were of three white men running downhill, but they had not survived their enemies this long by being careless. At the pass they made a long survey until they were certain everything below was just as they had seen it last. Still they took precautions. They tied the horses where Wolf had killed the guard, then her captor shoved her to the front of the line and as he passed the man carrying Pop Engle's rifle took it from him. He prodded her into the pass at the end of the short rope, the rifle held against her back. On the remote chance that the white men were in the bowl she would be shot as quickly as any of them fired. In that fashion they turned down the final grade.

When he had tucked the map inside his shirt Loco Smith had left the shelter and gone out to plot their strategy, beckoning Lambert down from the shoulder.

"How come?" Garrison had asked. "If that's not where you wanted him why'd you send him up in the first place?"

"Would you want him where he could look under that skin, watch us with the map? What he don't know won't hurt us."

"Do we give Albert a gun now?"

"I wouldn't. I don't think he's real fond of us and I want to concentrate on Indians. Lambert's enough to have to watch."

They had left Ned Albert hidden in the shelter. Garrison crouched behind rocks in the middle of the bowl. Craig Lambert was posted on a shelf below the gap. Loco was near the top just under the pass.

He was in position to hear the first approach of the Apaches. He would signal Lambert and Garrison, then drop part way down the slope and move north away from the pass opposite Lambert, but above him so he would not be a tempting target himself. Garrison was to open fire first. The Indians with only one gun could be expected to turn back and flee up the path but Loco and Lambert would by then be behind them and catch them in a cross fire between the three of them.

It had been a long, tense wait, but now Wolf Garrison was

117

vindicated. Five Apaches appeared in the pass. Only the wolf could see them. Loco and Lambert were keeping down out of sight until the red men should go by them. Wolf watched, impatient but the Indians were in no hurry to enter the valley. They were on foot and Garrison heaved a relieved sigh when they pushed Jerry Dillman alive and walking, out ahead of them.

Then he saw the rope. He saw the gun trained on her at the same time. The Indians were being very cautious, using her as a shield, lined out single file behind her, crouched. The wolf groaned. At the distance he dared not fire without the risk of hitting her.

Moving slowly they came down the path and with every step they were lower behind the girl. Loco heard them pass him and go on toward Lambert's position. He lifted his head to see and the sight froze him. He stood powerless, watching the little caravan pass thirty feet from him. He knew Wolf Garrison was just as helpless with Jerry between him and the Indians and he did not dare fire himself. He could hit the man with rifle in Jerry's back without hitting her, but if he did the Apache's finger might convulse on the trigger.

He lifted the gun, aimed at the retreating back, trying to think of a way of distracting the Indian's attention to make him shift the gun away from Jerry. Then he saw Craig Lambert rise from his hiding place below and steal to the lip of the ledge, saw Lambert's moment of hesitation, then the man laid his rifle aside and pulled his knife. The girl was passing directly beneath him as Lambert bent his knees.

Loco saw he meant to jump, but again, if he landed on the Apache the gun could still go off. If it did Jerry Dillman was as good as dead with a shattered spine. He opened his mouth and threw a high cry at the rear of the column.

It worked. All five Apaches spun to see who was behind them and in that second Lambert launched himself off the twenty-foot-high shelf, yelling at the girl.

"Drop, Jerry, drop."

Loco was dismayed. While the Indian with the gun was looking uphill he could have safely shot him, but the instant was lost. Lambert had landed on the Apache, knocked him to the ground but they were sprawled against the girl and now the other four swarmed around them, Jerry Dillman lying under their feet.

Loco could only watch. Lambert's knife flashed as the man under him twisted and swung the rifle barrel at his head. The blow missed and Lambert's knife sunk between the ribs. As the Apache fell back another jumped, slashing with a blade. Lambert took that on his left arm, a cut to the bone, but it did not stop him. He grabbed the bony wrist and yanked and as the savage fell toward him jackknifed his knee into the groin. The Indian doubled up in pain and Lambert plunged his knife into the exposed back.

Jerry Dillman had been admirably quick, rolling on the rifle and hugging it with both arms and legs. The three Indians remaining were too busy trying to get at Lambert to even see it.

Wolf Garrison came loping in, swinging his long gun around his head, clubbing right and left, cracking the stock against a chin as Loco scrambled down to join the battle. The man Wolf had hit tried to use his knife and Wolf swung the gun again, caught the side of the head and drove him back. The Indian fell, rolled and vanished into the tumbled rocks.

Loco was locked with the last two Indians in a fight that spun them all around and around so that he still could not shoot. One brown hand grabbed his hair, trying to pull Loco's head back for a thrust at his throat. The other got an arm under his chin. Loco wrenched aside, used both hands to force the arm up and bit it until his teeth hit bone.

The savage howled and let go. Lambert had had trouble pulling his knife out of the back he had sunk it in. It had grazed a rib and stuck there. Now he had it free and lunged at the Indian Loco had bit, sinking the blade into the hard side.

The Apache fell forward, arms flinging around Loco, taking him to the ground under him.

The last Indian had let go of Loco's hair and, while Wolf's and Lambert's attention was on Loco's fall, had dived after the one who made the rocks.

Lambert bent to help Loco break out of the death struggle of the man clinging to him but Loco shouted at him.

"The horses. . . . Get to the horses before they do. Stay with them."

Lambert whirled, snatched up Loco's rifle and pounded toward the pass. He was barely in time. The Apache who had escaped ambush first was sliding down the rocks. Another minute and he would have been aboard a horse. He snapped a shot on the run, missed the man and heard the bullet whine off stone, then the Indian was gone again like a red shadow.

Craig's impulse was to go after him but he decided it would be no use. This was the Apache's world and they knew how to live in it, melting out of sight as if the ground opened up and took them in without a sound. His boots would warn the man exactly where he was. He would either be jumped on from behind and stabbed or the savage would circle around him, grab a horse and be away while Lambert was searching for him.

Why Loco had told him to stay here he did not know, but there must be good reason for Smith to think of the order while he was fighting for his life. Staying and breathing the reeking air though was more than his stomach would take. Watching for movement in the rocks he raised his bandana over his nose, took a rope from a saddle, made a hitch around the foot of a mule, dallied it around a boulder at the edge of the trail and dragged the carcass until it balanced over the rim, cut the rope near the hoof so the stinking body fell. He dropped the other animal, then went into the pass and sat down against the wall where he could see the horses and not be surprised.

He was badly winded from the fight, the uphill run and the effort of hauling the mules. He sucked in deep, controlled breaths, willing steadiness into the hands that shook with reaction. He worried about Jerry Dillman, what she had been through. Her long blond hair hung in ratted strings, her face was white under the grime and marked with dark scratches.

Seeing her stumble down the trail, hands tied behind her, on a rope and with a rifle against her back he had gone berserk. Attacking five Indians armed with long knives was insanity. Under any other circumstances he would not have tried it. Only that voice yelling just before he jumped, making the Indians turn, had saved him. Whose voice was it? It had come from up the canyon but there was no one there. The rumors of the weird sights and sounds, the mysteries of the Superstitions came to his mind, but he shrugged them off. He was no believer in the supernatural.

But it was a puzzle. Perhaps Loco Smith in the rocks above and across from him had an explanation. He made a mental note to ask. With the action passed and time now to take stock he examined the cut on his arm. It was deep and hurting but it did not cripple him. He took off his bandana, shook out the gravel ground into it in his fall and tied it around the wound that still leaked blood, watching the precious horses rather than what his fingers did.

He had been there an hour, unable to see through the pass into the valley to tell what Loco and the wolf were doing about Jerry Dillman. He did not trust them alone with her much more than he trusted Apaches, but at least he could hear her if she screamed. There were no screams. There was no other sound, and tension built high as he waited for another try by the Indians.

Then he saw it, the shadow moving out from behind rocks down where the Apache had vanished. He raised the rifle, tightened his finger on the trigger and waited for the savage to appear. The shadow stopped before the man came into sight. Wolf Garrison called.

"Lambert? You there?"

Craig Lambert let out his pent up breath and lowered the gun. "Yes. You nearly got yourself shot. I thought your shadow was an Apache."

"I figured. Get the itch out of your finger so I can come down."

"Come ahead. What are you doing there?"

Garrison stepped out beside the horses and walked to Lambert. "What do you think? Looking for Indians. They must have moved up higher because they're not around here or I'd smell them."

"I'm glad to hear it. . . . Wolf, just before I jumped did you hear somebody yell up this way?"

"Yeah." The wolf was innocence itself. "That last bronco in the line spotted you and let out a whoop. I saw him look up at you."

Lambert accepted the words but he was not quite satisfied. His mind's eye recalled the picture he felt sure he had seen and all five Indians had been looking behind them while he was in the air. Still, Garrison's explanation was the only logical answer.

The wolf was saying something more and Lambert let go of the puzzle to listen.

"Loco took Jerry down to the shelters and I'm going to keep prowling around this hill. You stay here and mind these animals."

"Why don't we take them to the valley? They'll be safer there."

Garrison sounded disgusted. "Sure. But those broncos aren't going to show up where they'll get shot at. They might take a chance on slipping in here. Get yourself out of sight, they won't come with you parked out here holding that rifle."

Lambert flushed and looked for a less conspicuous position, one where he could see the animals and at the same time see a shadow if an Indian came close enough above him to throw a knife. The Superstitions were getting to him at that and he knew that he had unconsciously chosen the open pass because of a tingling fear of the silent, wraith-like denizens who could make themselves so invisible so quickly.

He climbed into a rock burst where the sun was at his back and watched Wolf Garrison hold the mane of a horse and throw himself onto its bare back and kick it up toward the jagged peaks, deliberately inviting the Indians. The more he saw of the man the more he suspected he really had Apache blood. He might actually have lived with the tribe and Wolf could be the translation of the name the Indians called him.

Wolf Garrison rode with care, hoping the animal under him would tempt the broncos to come for it. Horses were very important to them, both for transportation and as food when they were too used up to ride. He would cruise around until sunset but go back to the valley before dark.

With Craig Lambert perched on the crest and the wolf off making bait of a horse, Loco Smith congratulated himself. He cut the thong and rope off Jerry Dillman and left her lying in the trail to rest while he collected the crop of knives dropped by the Indians and broke Pop Engle's rifle. With two Apaches somewhere near the fewer weapons they could get their hands on the better he would like it. He stowed the knives in the back of his belt, then he knelt beside the girl and lifted her against his knee, holding her there.

Tears made muddy streaks on her face and there was still horror in her blue eyes. Loco kept his voice very soft.

"Are you hurt, Jerry? More than scratched and bruised?"

Instead of answering she twisted to her knees, wrapped her arms around him and held him tightly, lifted her head and pressed her lips against his mouth in a long, shuddering kiss. Loco returned it with enthusiasm. She was not practiced in the art but that made it all the sweeter to him. When they got out of here he would teach her himself. He had one arm around her soft body, one hand holding her chin against his, still tasting the warm mouth when she went limp and sagged against him.

He lifted her and carried her unconscious down to the shelter where Ned Albert hid, laid her in the shade and reached for the water skin. It was almost empty. He lifted her head, poured a little through her lips and used the rest on her face and around her neck until her eyes opened slowly.

He smiled down on her. She tried to smile back but it was a shaky attempt. To cheer her he told her, "Good news, honey. Uncle Ned Albert over there gave your map back to me. So when you're rested and we get those last two Indians off our necks we'll go dig up your pot of gold. You sleep some while I look for more water."

He liked the way her eyes lighted just before she closed them and fell asleep and he went back to the hot sun humming. It did not take long to find the well the Apaches had dug and walled with stone. The water level was four feet down but there was a clay olla with a rawhide rope. He dropped it, twitched the rope to sink the vessel and pulled it up full, about two gallons. Taking it back he built a fire, made a nest of stones and set the olla on that. While it heated he cut the hide from one shelter, carved out a circle and an oblong strip and laced them together for a bucket. It would leak some but would hold enough to fill the Indian water skin, a good-sized animal bladder. With the skin and the bucket he went again to the well.

There was soap plant up on the rock shoulder. Loco climbed and gathered a handful of the hard shiny buttons on the ground around the cactus and back at the camp pounded them to a coarse flour. When the water was hot he stripped and had his first bath since Phoenix. The girl should look with favor on that.

He had the olla filled and smoking again by the time Jerry Dillman waked. Albert had crawled out to ask for it but Loco made him wait a later turn. The girl sat up, then came out to the fire and looked enviously at Loco Smith's scrubbed head and face.

"Thought you might feel better with a bath," he told her, wrapped the soap powder in his bandana, filled the bucket with steaming water and carried them to the shelter farthest away, telling her about the cleansing properties of the plant seeds. "The Indian women use it to wash their hair. It works fine."

She followed him under the hide roof but drew back from the bandana with a shiver. "I don't want anything to do with anything Indian."

He laughed, saying, "They didn't make it, Jerry. It grows wild. You're as entitled to it as anybody. Go ahead, get out of your clothes. I'll stand guard outside so one of those broncos can't slip up on you."

"Loco . . ." She stopped him as he started to leave. "Thank you for everything. I owe you more than I'll ever be able to repay."

"We'll manage that together later."

He did not elaborate. He would feel less safe than he did now if she showed a favoritism for him before the wolf and Lambert. He went out, posted himself in front of the entrance and turned his back but a little later looked over his shoulder. Jerry Dillman was facing the back of the shelter dropping her riding clothes and stepping out of them and Loco Smith saw no reason not to enjoy her white beauty while she washed until a movement should warn him she was going to look his way.

CHAPTER 14

Craig Lambert had never thought he would be glad of Wolf Garrison's company, but he was when the outlaw came down to the pass after sunset. The pressure of the afternoon tension, of expecting a dark shape to appear suddenly at any moment had taken a toll. His guns and his ability to use them were reassurances, but not comfort enough in this land where any movement meant danger, where the peaks were like giant teeth waiting to clamp on him and the sun was a battering ram.

Wolf's voice, calling before he came into sight, lifted the crushing weight off Lambert's shoulders and he was almost friendly when the tall, dark man dropped off the horse.

"You didn't find either of them I judge. I haven't heard a shot. Do you think they gave up and left?"

"An Apache quit? While there are horses here? Don't you believe it. They'll be after them tonight."

Lambert had a bad moment thinking Garrison intended leaving the animals on this ridge where the shadowlike men could slip through the night and drive them off before they were seen. But Garrison lifted a saddle, threw it on a fresh animal and hung a pack bag on the horn, saying,

"Load up, Lambert, we take everything down now."

Craig Lambert saddled the horses and draped the bags on them while the wolf kept watch. If the broncos were looking they just could try a raid before the animals were taken out of this more vulnerable location. But there was no attempt and they took the string through the pass and down to the camp.

Ned Albert kept to the shade of the shelter, unarmed and sulking. Loco Smith and Jerry Dillman sat shoulder to shoulder against a boulder with the fresh deck of cards he had picked up in Phoenix, Loco teaching poker to the girl.

Lambert and Wolf dismounted, both scowling at the pair. Where they were sweated and dirt streaked Loco's skin shone clean and the mat of mud was gone from his beard. The girl was washed, even her hair, and the long golden strands were braided, coiled high on her head and pinned with cactus thorns. On the ground beside her lay a comb with six short teeth Loco had carved from a length of a rib of a horse the Apache had shot.

The Indian bodies in the valley had been dragged to the cluster of dead animals. There was a fire with an olla of water steaming over it. A water skin hung full in the mouth of a shelter where shade and breeze would keep it coolest. Loco Smith, Lambert decided, had been very busy indeed at impressing Jerry Dillman.

Wolf Garrison got off his mount, his eyes narrowed, saying, "Lambert, unsaddle the horses, and Loco, take them out and picket them over where that dry grass is."

He was at the fire before Craig Lambert was on the ground, catching the olla by the rawhide line coiled on top of it and crossing to sweep up the comb.

Loco said laconically, "There's a wash bucket in that far shelter. You'll smell better after you use it."

He winked at the girl, put the cards in her hand, took the reins of the two horses Lambert had unsaddled and led them into an open space where a thin mat of sun-cured grass lay, hobbled them and went back for the others.

By the time he was finished the wolf was bathed and brushed, his black hair wet and gleaming with blue highlights, digging into the packs. Hurried when they had killed Gilbert Engle and taken Jerry and the horses, the Indians had not torn into the packs and the remains of their food supply was still there. Wolf laid out jerked meat and hard biscuits and a handful of coffee beans.

"Loco, can you get another jug of water? I judge there's plenty."

"A well full. Use the skin for coffee while I'm filling this."

Craig Lambert fumed. There seemed nothing to be done that these two did not beat him to. He was at a disadvantage in this desert country, unfamiliar with the lore of existing on plants he knew nothing about, and until he could bathe as they had done the comparison kept him well away from the blond girl. After the long hike on the Indians' trail he was as rank as the savages themselves.

Wolf Garrison unpacked the coffeepot, set it over the coals, ground the beans between stones, brushed them into his palm and added them to the water. He took the frying pan, reached for Jerry's hand and pulled her to her feet.

"Come on and see how they make bread in these parts."

With these men around her again Jerry felt secure from the Indians even if two were still somewhere in the mountains, on foot and with only knives, and her curiosity was returning. The wolf took her to a mound of loose dirt, raked it away with the side of his hand and uncovered a shallow pit. A thick layer of dough was spread over rocks the size of a fist that had been heated to make an oven. They were cold now but the dough was baked hard. Wolf worked it loose from the stones, brushed off most of the dirt and dropped it in the pan.

"Agave bread," he told her. "From that cactus with the big thick leaves the whites call a century plant. You make the dough out of the pulp, bake it twenty-four hours and this is what you get. Boil the same pulp a lot longer and it makes a liquor, mescal, that gives you dreams like nothing you ever knew."

They took it back to the fire and heated it. The girl was revolted at the idea of eating anything the Indians had made but there was not enough left of the food they had brought and she must have nourishment. Wolf called Ned Albert out and divided the agave between the five of them. It was dry, bitter, but palatable.

Chewing on the bread and the thin, stringy strips of dried meat, the biscuits soaked in coffee, they took the edge off their hunger, but they would have to find another source of food the next day.

When he finished Wolf Garrison took Loco's bucket and the horses two at a time to the well, watered them and hobbled them on a different plot of grass. Only then did Craig Lambert have the opportunity to use the vessel and hot water, and not until he was as clean as he could make himself did he go to Jerry Dillman.

Ned Albert had gone back under the hide roof, feeling safer than near the men with guns and Loco Smith had taken a blanket into another shelter to sleep while Garrison stood watch. Lambert crouched at the girl's side.

"Jerry, can you talk about it . . . while the Indians had you?"

She had been trying to put that time out of her mind but it rushed back at his question and she began to shake.

"It was awful, Craig. They put me on a horse in front of one of them and he had his arm around me holding me against him all the way. They made me eat rattlesnake . . . then one tried to rape me but the others wouldn't let him. They meant to bring me here first. Oh, Craig. . . ." She began to cry and buried her head against his shoulder. "If you hadn't been here . . . if you hadn't made that dangerous jump . . . what would have happened . . . ?"

He held her in his arms, stroking her hair, aching to comfort her. "It was a crazy thing to do, Jerry. I lost my head when I saw you. I should have waited until they thought they were safe and took the rifle off you. Then we could have shot them."

He needed sleep himself if he was to be any help through the night but she was trembling so much he could not let her go. He lifted her face and kissed her and with his mouth on hers pulled her down to the ground and lay with her head on his arm. In a very short time they were both asleep.

Loco Smith saw them when he got up at dusk, passed them without waking them and walked to Garrison. Wolf had moved the horses again.

"That lawman has to go soon, Wolf. Jumping like he did made him a hero to Jerry and right now they're curled up spoon fashion, cozy as can be."

"We'll get to him in time but we still need him until we find that box, don't we? There's bound to be more than this one bunch of broncos in here."

"I guess. First thing is to get the two we know about."

"I aim to tonight. They're up in those rocks watching us. We've got their well and their bread and horses, and I'm rubbing their noses in it so they'll make a pass for the animals when it's good and dark."

"You're telling it. How do you think they'll do it?"

"Put yourself in their place. You've got a knife but no gun and you know we'll have a sentry with a rifle guarding these animals. You have to draw the guard off so you show yourself, act like your leg is broken maybe and you can't run fast so he'll take after you and give the other bronco time to drive the horses up through the gap."

"But we'll have a surprise for them."

"We will. One of us will be on guard in sight by the fire. He lets himself be drawn away. The other of us is hidden here by the horses and as soon as the Indian shows up he gets shot."

"Sounds easy. You'd better get a little sleep while it gets dark."

"I don't need it, I slept day before yesterday. Let's get back to camp while they can see us."

CHAPTER 15

Dark settled in the bowl and worked up the hillside. Jerry Dillman and Craig Lambert slept in each other's arms and Ned Albert slept under the hide roof. Loco had taken a blanket to the farthest shelter and gone in, waited until the night was black enough, then gone to hide near the hobbled horses. They stood with their heads drooping, worn out by the day's long ride.

The wolf had chosen to be the decoy guard. "I can follow him better than you, Loco," he had explained. "I know, he expects to pull me out of the way and then lose me in the rocks but that's another surprise he'll get. He's not going to lose me."

Loco had not argued. He had as much experience as Wolf with Apaches but he preferred the less strenuous task of waiting for a horse thief to come to him.

The night wore on and the horses gave no sign of smelling Indian. Time was crowding Loco. It was getting close to moonrise and if it came over the mountain before the Indians slipped in he might be discovered by a shaft reflecting off his gun. To prevent that he took off his shirt and ran the barrel through a sleeve.

The glow in the sky grew. Then the silence was broken by a stone rattling down the slope. The wolf jumped to his feet and ran toward the sound and ahead of him other stones rattled after the first as if the Indian was careless in his haste to get out of range. Wolf started climbing the wall of the shoulder making his own noise so his Indian could tell he was being chased.

The combined clatter waked Lambert and Jerry Dillman, and Lambert started up, his head swiveling, looking for whoever was on guard and not seeing one grabbed his rifle, pushed the girl into the shelter farthest from the fire and planted himself in front of her.

At the horses Loco did not see the savage materialize beside them. He only knew the man was there because the animals began rearing on their picket lines, circling and snorting. He stood up quietly, waiting for a target, saw a shadow move but before he could fire a horse danced in front of it. The picket line was cut and the animal galloped away. A second horse was cut loose and bolted and still the milling animals wheeled between Loco and the Indian. Loco put the rifle down, drew his side gun and ran into the melee as the moon lifted over the peaks and lighted the valley.

The Indian saw Loco coming, slashed a third line, caught the bridle and flung himself half up, hanging along the flank on the far side but instead of racing off the animal jumped at Loco. The jump brought it almost above him and Loco dodged to keep from being run down, turned his foot and lost his balance. In that instant the savage dropped off the animal and as it loped past dived for Loco Smith with his knife at arm's length, slashing.

With his gun hand flung out to catch himself there was no time to bring it around and fire. Loco swung it to deflect the knife, then before the point could reach for him again Loco slammed the barrel against the side of the Apache's head as hard as he could. Momentum carried the man on and he jarred into Loco, taking both of them down in a tangle. Loco's head cracked against a rock, stunning him and he dropped the gun.

Unable to move at the moment he watched the Indian roll to his knees, the knife raised and ready to be driven through Loco's throat. Galvanized by the threat Loco's arms shot up to catch the arm and the blade sliced across the back of his hand. It was raised again and Loco rolled just beyond the arc of the thrust, reaching for his own knife but it was underneath him and he could not pull it out. He yelled Lambert's name once, all he had time for.

The Indian jumped astraddle of him, the knees pinning Loco's arms, the knife over his head. Then a gun exploded. The Apache body jerked back, collapsed and the falling knife pricked into Loco's bare arm above the elbow, then fell away.

Loco lay panting with the Indian's weight across him until Craig Lambert walked into his sight, his smoking gun still in his hand with Jerry Dillman close beside him. Embarrassed before this particular girl without his shirt, Loco scrambled out from under the body and went to pull it off the rifle and shrug into it, then walked to where they waited.

Rather than thanking the lawman he said simply, "Nice shot, Lambert."

"Just returning the favor, Smith. You hauled some Indians off me a while back."

Jerry Dillman saw the dark blood running from Loco's hand, gasped and took the fingers to examine the cut, saying, "Craig, he's hurt."

Lambert did not sound too distressed. "Only a scratch. Some of Wolf's aloe will mend it. Loco, where is Garrison?"

"Up on the hill chasing the last Apache. This one cut three horses loose so we'll have to round them up before a cat locates them. Spooked as they are it's going to take the three of us. The one closest, over there, we'll go for first. Jerry, you move in on him from one side, Lambert from the other. Work him toward the wall. He'll try to run around or between you but don't let him."

They went to the camp for ropes, then herded the animal toward the wall. Prancing nervously it turned one way and then another but Jerry, waving her arms and Lambert swinging his coiled rope around his head kept it from running off on either side. When it was close to the rising grade it wheeled to make a dash back toward the valley and Loco, waiting for the move had a loop shaken out and dropped it over the head. It settled down quietly then, accustomed to these people, and he returned it to the picket.

The other two gave them more trouble. It was an hour before they had them rounded up and the body of the Indian dragged a hundred feet downwind where the odor would not keep the animals on edge. Loco was growing concerned about Wolf Garrison. There had been no shooting in the hills. If the wolf had overestimated his ability to track the Apache he could have been surprised and knifed and the red man still to be reckoned with.

That would eliminate Garrison from the contest for Jerry Dillman but it was not a solution Loco liked. Besides the Apache there was Ned Albert to think about. It was very possible that if the wolf did not come back Craig Lambert would give the man a gun without Loco knowing it, and if they got out of here and found the money those two were sure to gang up against him. No, he wanted Garrison alive.

They returned to the camp and built up the fire to heat coffee. With what little sleep he had had in so many hours Loco needed the stimulant to keep him awake until he could go look for Wolf in daylight.

Ned Albert was a dark shape lying in the shelter. Loco shook his head that the man showed no curiosity at all about Lambert's shot or the noise they had made gathering the horses, although he had been aware the Indians were expected. Loco headed for the water skin that had been left hanging at the entrance to add to the coffeepot. It was not there. He supposed Albert had taken it in with him and ducked under the low hide to look for it, struck a match, then crouched transfixed until it burned his fingers. Ned Albert's throat was cut and a circle of his scalp gone. So was the water skin.

Loco backed out and looked toward the fire. Jerry Dillman sat with her back to him, Lambert was on his feet facing him. He raised a hand and beckoned slowly with all four fingers. Lambert excused himself and came forward, puzzled by Loco's empty face. Loco stepped aside, nodded the lawman in and struck another match.

"Where were you and Jerry when that devil got in here?"

Craig Lambert let out a rasping breath and his voice shook. "Back in that last shelter. I didn't see him, didn't hear him. . . . He didn't come looking there."

"Got what he was after, water. Albert was a bonus. He was in a hurry for the horses."

A boot scraped on stone outside and Loco spun, saying, "Get rid of him," in a whisper, then raised his voice to the girl coming toward them. "Pick up the olla, Jerry, we have to go to the well."

In his sock feet Wolf Garrison climbed after the decoy Apache. The Indian left a noisy trail up through the rocks, following the curve of the valley away from the pass until the guard chasing him was above rifle range of the floor. Then he made no more sound. The wolf followed the spoor he left, twisting around the peaks and then across them where even a mountain goat could not get through. He trailed him a long way, then into a steep canyon he had not been in before and there the downdraft was strong, carrying the scent away, making a false trail.

The wolf stopped. He could not tell where the Indian was any longer and the odds were good that the man could wait down-wind until he passed and slip in from behind. Just as bad, the moon was coming and would pick out his movements. Garrison considered. The Indians were after the horses. The one in the valley intended to drive them out through the pass so the one he chased would probably go there to stop them from running on down the trail.

Wolf backtracked up the canyon where he was less apt to be surprised, then headed for the outside entrance to the gap. He was halfway there when the moon lighted the country and ahead of him and lower down he saw the Indian and knew his guess was right, but the glimpse was too brief to give him a shot, and he moved on.

With the rim of peaks between him and the valley to cut off sound he did not hear Lambert's shot, but when he got close to the gap there were shouts inside, the loose animals being caught. And the decoy stood in the trail below the wolf.

Wolf fired but the Indian moved just as he squeezed the trigger and he missed. The Apache ran, weaving and dodging behind boulders down the crooked trail. Wolf went after him, firing twice more without hitting him, and now the Indian knew there was a white man close behind.

He disappeared around a sharp turn with Wolf now less than a hundred yards away. The wolf ran toward it, then stopped abruptly at the rattle of rock ahead. That would be the man in a hurried scramble to get above the trail where he could drop on top of Garrison when he ran by.

The trail around the jutting corner was narrow and if the wolf turned it standing up he would be a prime target. Wolf lay down against the rock and wriggled forward, his head against the ground, looking up, until he could see beyond the curve. There the Indian crouched, fifteen feet above, his knife raised, intent on a spot six feet over Wolf's head.

Garrison crept back out of sight and stood up, raising his rifle to the height of the Indian's perch, put his back against the wall, then spun around it. The Apache was quick, launching himself at the wolf. He was in the air when Garrison shot him. The wolf dodged back and the body went past, landed on the lip of the trail, hung there, then rolled over the edge.

Garrison stepped across to look down. It was a long drop. Halfway to the bottom the body was spread-eagled across a boulder. It did not move but the wolf put two more shots into it for safety's sake. Then he turned back toward the pass.

Loco Smith went halfway up the path to meet him. It had to be Garrison doing the shooting because if an Indian had got hold of his gun he'd have come down where he could snipe from the rocks with a chance of hitting something.

"I judge you got your bronco," Loco said. "What took you so long?"

Garrison's feet were sore from the sharp rocks digging through his socks and the spines of a pancake cactus he had stepped on and he said sourly, "We played some cards to see who won the gun. What about yours?"

"I hate to admit it but he'll tell you if I don't. Lambert had to bail me out. There's other news. While you were chasing your boy and I was waiting for mine he detoured into camp after water, saw Albert and killed him, took the scalp. . . ."

"Jerry," the wolf interrupted. "Is she all right?"

"Yeah. When you went up the hill Lambert took her into a shelter and stood guard but my Apache didn't take the time to check it out, didn't show up there. He told her about Albert and now he's a bigger hero than before."

"That guy. He has to be the luckiest bastard in all Arizona."

"Luck runs out," Loco Smith said. "We've got a ways to go yet and we're making headway. We've got the map and Albert and the Indians are out of the way. Lambert's day will come."

Craig Lambert was getting in too many counters with the girl to please Wolf Garrison but when he and Loco reached the camp he felt that he was still in equal contention for her favor. She ran to him, lovely in the moonlight, and took both his hands, holding them.

"Wolf, thank Heaven you're back safe. I was so worried. You were so long I was afraid that Indian had caught you."

Lambert came up, sounding less enthusiastic. "If we lost you and a rain washed out the tracks I wouldn't know how to get out of this maze."

Wolf smiled on the girl without telling Lambert that the likelihood of rain at this season was in the realm of miracle. He limped to the fire, filled the leather bucket with warm water to soak his burning feet and was further rewarded when Jerry Dillman sat on the ground in front of him and tenderly picked out all the cactus thorns she could feel.

Loco Smith told Lambert, "You keep watch the rest of the night so a cat doesn't get to the horses."

He did not believe there was much chance any prowling animal would come this close to humans and a fire, but it was a way of making the lawman suffer the loss of a full sleep. For himself he poured a last cup of coffee. It hardly deserved the name since the same grounds had been boiled four times but the heat felt good in his empty stomach.

It was high time they left this place and found some food. There was more of the baked mescal but it was too pithy for Loco's taste. What he needed was meat. They might find a deer along the way or a snake, or if it came to the worst they could eat a horse and Jerry could ride double. That was in fact a pleasant prospect even if he had to share her in the interest of peace until they had the money.

Loco had eaten horse before. It was a little soft and too sweet, did not have the grain of beef. Then there was his distaste for eating an animal he staked his life on. It was a practicality, not a sentiment. He did not recognize a rapport between a man and his horse. The animal was not like a dog that loved its master, it let a man, almost any man, ride it because it had been broken to accept a rider.

CHAPTER 16

Jerry Dillman had very mixed emotions about leaving the little valley in the morning. She had known dread coming into it as a captive and fear until all of the Apaches were killed. She had seen too much of death in this place and the sights and smells of it would haunt her vividly. And yet it was here Craig Lambert had proved how much he loved her, throwing himself down upon more Indians than any one man could survive, and in that moment she had learned the depth of her love for him.

That was enough to make this bowl dear to her, but there was more. Loco Smith and Wolf Garrison had proven great courage, risking their lives again and again for her sake. How could anyone be so fortunate as to have men of their caliber for friends. She felt an especial love for each of them, different from that she had for Lambert but just as deep. She had ridden into the Superstitions with strangers, in ignorant innocence that appalled her now, and they had kept her safe from harm. She was riding out with the sure conviction of the goodness of these men.

She watched their preparations for leaving, Loco watering the horses, filling the canteens. Craig saddling the animals as Loco brought them up. Wolf Garrison making up the packs that each would carry, digging up the rest of the several agave ovens to take the bread along, each doing some necessary chore of his own volition in silence, no one giving orders to another.

Then they lined out, Garrison ahead, then Loco, herself behind him and Craig following her, still careful to shield her, watchful of the hills as they had been at first.

At the ridge above the canyon where he had seen the deer the wolf stopped them and went on alone. In a little while there was a shot and then his call. When they came up he was skinning out a doe. Loco made a fire and they roasted the liver, ate and took the haunches with them. The food made a difference in their spirits, lightened them all.

The return trip was much shorter than the one in. They did not follow the Alberts' long detour from where the false burial spots had stopped but went more directly there. Still it took them the better part of two days because the horses were faltering. They had been short of forage in the Superstitions, their ribs showed and their wind was short.

Wolf rode with a faraway look, recalling the shapes of the rocks they had passed, and none of them reminded him of a horse head. Loco could not remember seeing one either.

They were nearly down to the head of Broken Ax Canyon when Smith said, "Wolf, which way does that rock face? We know Dillman went a lot farther up than we are now so it could face this way and we haven't come to it, but maybe it does face the way we came in. We didn't know what to look for so we could have missed it. We might have to go all the way to the bottom and come back again."

"Could be. You got anything better to do with your time?"

"Nothing I like better than riding around this kind of place looking for that box."

The trail was wide enough that they rode side by side, Loco watching one wall and Wolf the other. A mile on down Wolf put a hand across to Loco's knee and reined in. Loco looked toward him as Wolf said,

"Over there. What do you see?"

Forty feet across the canyon a pillar rose out of the hillside, standing alone, a cap rock overhanging the top. Looking down-trail at it the cap rock had two stone upright ears and the long muzzle of a horse's outstretched head.

Wolf backed his animal two feet and the illusion vanished. He went forward two feet ahead of Loco and the head was lost again. Behind them Jerry and Lambert hauled up and the girl called,

"What are you looking at?"

Garrison waved her to him and positioned her, pointing. "Here we are, blondie. Here's where we get rich. That rock up there."

Jerry Dillman gasped in dismay, her blue eyes widening. "But it's so high. How could anybody climb that thing?"

Loco Smith brought out the map and read the full text aloud with an audible tremor in his voice.

Find the rock that looks like a horse head. Go to it and turn west into the draw under it for twenty-five steps. There is a cave hollowed out by wind. Dig away the rubble that looks like a natural rockslide. The money box is buried there.

Craig Lambert rode in, listening, watching, very quiet. A tension held them all. In silence they dismounted and walked to the pillar and into the draw. The three men paced off the steps to the west, Jerry Dillman following but not able to keep stride, Loco Smith carrying the miner's shovel salvaged from the mule packs. The walls of the draw were sheer at the prescribed location and there was plenty of rubble at the foot of them, but there was no cave, not even a shallow undercut. They walked farther but did not find it.

Saying nothing, Loco Smith turned about, went back to the pillar and began pacing east. Wolf Garrison called after him.

"That's not west . . . the map says west."

At twenty-five paces Loco stopped and pointed. Above the heap of stones and coarse sand against the wall a smooth curve of rock depression made a half moon.

As Wolf ran to him Loco said, "Dillman must have been turned around, or maybe he was as devious as Gilbert said, wrote it backward on purpose."

He threw the shovel to Garrison and started throwing stones as large as his head off the pile, saying, "Start shoveling if you want a piece of this gold mine."

Garrison shoveled the loose sand with a fury of will, looking often at Jerry Dillman where she hung on Craig Lambert's arm bright eyed and barely breathing, her red lips parted like a child before a Christmas tree.

Lambert watched the labor with a special tension. If the box was actually here, filled with Wells Fargo money, this day marked the end of the longest manhunt of his career. He had not taken Dillman or Gilbert alive, but they would rob no more trains or stages and he would recover for the company much that they had stolen from it.

Yet that brought him face to face with what would now be unavoidable. Telling Jerry Dillman the money was not hers, that he was a special agent assigned to claim it for the express firm. How would she react? Would she turn from love to hating him and he lose her? If as he had at first suspected she knew it was stolen her reaction would tell him for certain and he could hold her perfidy before his mind until desolation healed, but if she was truly innocent how could he ever tolerate the loss of her?

Still moving stones, Loco kept one eye on Lambert. If they found the box and he knew it that would be the moment he would make his play, throw down on him and the wolf to grab the jackpot of the treasure and two prisoners, and he said in a low voice to Garrison, "Work your shovel down as if you're loosening the ground and if you hit wood or metal keep quiet about it but let me know. I don't want that lawman jumping us."

Garrison gave no sign he heard but began probing with the shovel blade, working it deeper until the blade was out of sight. The tip touched something that was not rock and stopped with a faint clink. Both of them heard it. Their eyes passed the message and Loco straightened, arching his back with a hand against it, looking at Lambert.

"Come over here and spell me with these things, they're heavy."

Lambert hesitated. He did not want to be that close to the outlaws if the box was found, but Jerry Dillman said, "Help them, Craig, I can't hold my breath much longer."

He did not know how to refuse without rousing suspicion. He would have to risk their beating him to a draw and trust his own speed, which was fast, so he walked to the rubble and bent, picked up a rock in both hands and was lifting it when Loco brushed close to him and slipped his gun out of the holster. Lambert would not have felt it except for the lightened weight as his belt. He dropped the rock and stood stiff.

"What's that about, Smith?"

Loco smiled and tucked the gun under his belt, stepping back, and said mildly, "Looking at a lot of money can make people try crazy stunts. You might decide you want it all. Go on, let's see what's down there."

Lambert's stomach was cold. He had no illusion about these men. If the treasure was found they would kill him and without a gun he could not prevent it. And if they killed him would they leave Jerry alive to tell it? Through the whole trip both of them had showed an infatuation with her but he could not believe either would put her life above his own. Yet they might not shoot him in front of her, and it could be that if there were a box to open greed would keep their concentration on that long enough that he could reach the rifle on his horse.

Stiffly he bent to the job of uncovering whatever was in the ground here. Garrison was shoveling faster and that told him he had been tricked, they had already discovered something. He cursed himself that thinking about Jerry Dillman had made him so careless.

He had the big rocks cleared away. The wolf's shovel clanged on metal and scraped sand aside and the dull corner of a Wells Fargo chest appeared. A long, rasping sigh from Garrison and Smith blended into a single sound and they looked transfixed by the sight. Very slowly Lambert took one backward step and then another.

Without looking away from the corner of the box Loco Smith waggled a beckoning finger. "Don't leave now," he said casually. "Don't you want to see what's in it? Give the wolf a hand."

That chance was lost, and would there come another? If he could signal Jerry to bring his rifle it just might. He looked toward her and called.

"It's here . . . bring up my horse to drag it out."

The girl whirled toward the animals but Loco stopped her.

"Never mind, we'll manage it. Come have a look."

Lambert's options were running out. So was time. Garrison had the top of the box cleared and was working down toward the handles. The girl ran to him, catching Lambert's arm in both hands, her fingers digging deep expressing without words her emotion that she, who had never had more than a meager living, was about to share with him half of a fortune she could not conceive of. Lambert put the hands away, rougher than he liked, but he needed his body free to move.

The girl looked hurt, then she read the lettering stenciled on the box, WELLS FARGO and was bewildered, asking,

"Where would my father get a Wells Fargo money box?"

With that tone Craig Lambert's last doubt was swept away and his eyes filled with pain. Loco Smith read it plainly, understood and smiled. He felt positive now with the man's reluctance to help dig out the box that he was an agent and he was going to enjoy watching Lambert tell Jerry Dillman what he finally had to. That should effectively turn her against him so that memory of him would not stand in the way of an arrangement between her and himself. It was a pleasure to see the outright pleading in the lawman's eyes, asking Loco's permission to take her aside and he nodded. It would not help his cause if he were to hear her shamed.

Lambert did not lead her toward the horses. Loco Smith would not let him do that. He took her down the draw out of earshot and faced her.

"I'd rather cut my tongue out than tell you this, Jerry. Your father stole the box and everything in it. He and Pop Engle were highwaymen who hit Wells Fargo hard."

"Oh no." It was a gasp. "What makes you say that?"

"I am a special agent for the company. I've been hunting your father for years."

She backed away, thoughts racing across her face, losing color. "And that is the reason you are here. . . . You followed me from Denver to find him. . . . You don't love me at all. . . . You're just using me."

"No I'm not, Jerry." Urgency choked him. "It started that way, yes. I thought you were going to meet him. I had to follow you. It was my job. But after I knew you. . . . Please understand."

In a dead voice she said, "Oh, I understand, Mr. Lambert. Just take the money and go away and my compliments on your acting."

"Damn the money. I can't take it away from you now. Jerry, I love you too much to let it come between us." It was the first time in his life Lambert had backed away from duty and he was too stricken to care.

"I don't want it. I didn't know it was stolen. I didn't know about my father."

146

Tears choked her voice and she started to run. He caught her by a hand and pulled her back.

"I'm sure you didn't. And you don't know what danger you are in here. Believe this, Jerry, Smith and Garrison mean to take that money and kill me and they've got my gun. Get to the horses and bring mine while they're opening the chest so I can reach my rifle."

She jerked the hand free, looked at him with utmost scorn and ran straight to the wolf and Loco.

Loco winked at Garrison and waved Lambert in, and when the agent walked heavily to them smiled at the girl while he told Lambert, "Grab a handle. You and Wolf haul the box out in the draw."

Sick with dread for the girl Lambert hauled. Wells Fargo boxes were heavy empty and he had experience enough to know that this one was too light. Wondering, he stood back.

"Go ahead, Wolf," Loco said. "Blow her open."

The wolf put his gun against the big padlock and pulled the trigger. The lock shattered. Wolf holstered his gun, took hold of the hasp and tipped the lid back. In the bottom lay two pearl-handled revolvers. There was nothing else inside.

CHAPTER 17

Loco Smith looked from one blank face to another across the heavy silence, then drew in and exhaled a deep breath. He had lost gambles before and recovered. He would survive this one. And there was still the girl. That much he was sure of.

Explanations of why there was no money ran through his mind. Mame Carter at the Phoenix hotel had written the letter to Pop Gilbert because Dillman was too weak to do it himself. Perhaps she had drawn the map under his direction and used it herself before keeping her promise to mail it. She would have needed the help of only one man. Perhaps it had been Carney who had killed Dillman. They had found no trace of him but he could have found the treasure, loaded it on a mule string and buried the empty box to be found by Pop Engle. He might have been caught by Indians and killed before he got out of the Superstitions. The Apaches despised money and would have abandoned it and it was lost to everyone.

Loco put the speculations aside and walked to Jerry Dillman, standing as far from Craig Lambert as she could get and still see into the box, dropping his hands on her shoulders with a twisted smile.

"Some you win and some you lose, honey. I'm sorry, but it isn't fatal. We'll make out."

Wolf Garrison was not to be left out of that picture and hurried to join them with his own commiserations and comfort. Loco and the wolf were so busy sparring for her attention that they paid no attention to Lambert except to note that he was still beside the empty chest, on one knee as if peering into it would fill it for him.

Craig Lambert was looking at the two very special thirty-eight revolvers. He was sure who they belonged to. These were James Hume's prized pair, taken from him when Dilly Dillman had held up the Tombstone stage. It was the loss of these that had made the head of the Wells Fargo police call Lambert from Montana and send him on the long trail after the outlaw.

Lambert did not wonder that whoever had recovered the fortune had chosen to leave the guns. They were famous through the West and anyone seen with one was asking for trouble from the company. He picked one up, hefted it for balance and broke it to see what shape the barrel was in. What he saw was all chambers loaded. He reached for the other and it, too, was filled.

Craig Lambert did not move a muscle for a long moment. He did not know how long these pistols had lain buried, whether the cartridges were too damp to fire, but the country was so bone dry it was possible they would still explode. There was only one way to find out.

He could not return the money to Hume and only give him the report that the two highwaymen he was so personally anxious to have in his custody were dead. But the disappointment could be mitigated if he could deliver Loco Smith and Wolf Garrison. Besides the satisfaction professionally the rewards offered for them would be enough to get married on if he could win back Jerry's faith. He stood up slowly and slowly turned to face them, only ten feet from them, and fired one shot at the ground to test the gun. The shell exploded.

He leveled both guns as the men spun away from the girl in astonishment. Loco Smith took half a step to put himself behind her and Lambert said sharply,

"Don't move, Smith. Unbuckle your belts, both of you, and throw them over here."

Loco arched his brows at Garrison and neither touched their belts. Lambert put another shot at Smith's feet and threw dirt over his boot. Loco yelped.

"You'll hit Jerry."

"Not at this distance. Drop those belts before I shoot the buckles out."

Looking at his face they believed him and without taking their eyes off his they took off the belts and threw them toward him.

"Now my gun, Loco, out of your pants, carefully."

Loco's blue eyes darkened but he tossed Lambert's gun among the others.

"Smith, get over against the wall and face it. Garrison, line yourself up between Smith and me and turn your back." When they were both in the sights of a single gun he gathered up those on the ground, holstered his and tossed the rest as far as he could toward the horses, saying, "Jerry, bring me two ropes from the saddles."

Her blue eyes very wide, she said shakily, "Whatever for?"

"So I can tie them. I told you they intended to kill me and probably you too. Jerry, these men escaped from Yuma prison. They were sent there for murder. They're wanted in every territory in the West for every crime in the book. I'm taking them back to Yuma."

She looked from Garrison to Smith, standing with shoulders drooping, then again to Lambert.

"They are no such thing, they're not who you think they

are. They saved your life and mine. They fought the Indians. They tracked them and rescued me. Bad men wouldn't do all that. Craig, you're mistaken."

"Oh no I am not. When we get to town I'll show you pictures of them on the sheriff's dodgers offering five thousand dollars for each of them. Dead or alive."

"Loco and Wolf? Outlaws? Well even if they are we owe them our lives and you can't repay them by taking them back to prison."

Lambert said doggedly, "I can and I will. You don't know what you're saying. Jerry, get the ropes."

There was a short silence. She did not move. Then a cry burst from her.

"Craig Lambert, do you want to marry me?"

Loco Smith took a chance and turned around and saw Lambert's face coming apart, heard his matching cry.

"You know I do, what's that got to do with these two?"

"A lot. I would never trust my happiness to a man with so little honor as to do a thing like you want to do."

For a second Lambert's whole attention was on the girl and in that second Loco mouthed a message to Wolf Garrison.

"Be ready to jump him."

The wolf did not dare nod but he winked. Loco pitched his voice beyond Lambert and threw an Apache war cry. The agent spun, emptying both pearl-handled guns at the space behind him before he saw no one was there.

Wolf Garrison was eight feet away. He pivoted and launched himself like a battering ram, hit Lambert between the shoulders and momentum drove Lambert to the ground with Wolf on top of him.

The jolt of Wolf's head and the fall knocked the wind out of Lambert and he dropped the guns, but he was quick, rolling out from under, rising to his knees and slapping at the gun in his holster.

Loco, diving close after the wolf, aimed a kick that caught

151

the gun as it cleared the leather and sent it flying into the rocks, scooped up one pearl-handled weapon and slammed it against Lambert's head. The man ducked, shoved to his feet but Garrison grabbed an ankle and brought him down again, let go the ankle and reached for the throat. Lambert forked his fingers and stabbed at Wolf's eyes and the wolf rolled away.

Lambert used the second to get on his feet, threw a fist at Loco that connected and knocked him down, then Garrison had the ankle again, twisting it, and Lambert fell heavily on his back. This time Garrison got a throttle hold. Lambert clawed with both hands, pried a finger out and back, snapping the bone.

Wolf yelled and let go. Lambert rolled away, got up and kicked hard at Garrison's ribs. Loco was circling, watching for an opening, and now jumped on Lambert's back, driving him down once more. The wolf shoved Loco away, wrapped his good hand around Lambert's neck again and clamped his thumb on the Adam's apple.

Lambert fought but he was tiring, strangling, his face reddening. Abruptly he went limp, unconscious. Wolf kept on squeezing.

Then Jerry Dillman was there, screaming, "You've all gone crazy. Stop it, Wolf."

Wolf did not stop and she picked up one of Hume's guns and beat on his dark head again and again, Loco wincing as he watched each blow until Garrison collapsed unconscious beside Lambert. She stood over them, her breast heaving, gasping in quick breaths.

Loco checked the pearl-handled guns, found them both empty and dropped them, went for his belt and buckled it around him, hung Garrison's on his saddle and hunted for Lambert's gun, shoving it in his waistband. Then he brought a rope to where Jerry sat, cradling Lambert's head in her lap.

He shoved Lambert's legs together and looped the rope around them. Jerry Dillman laid the head down and scrambled on her knees, sat on Lambert's ankles and snatched at the rope, trying to pull it away from Loco, gasping,

"No . . . No . . . Not you too. . . . What's happened to you?"

He let her have the rope, smiling, and said quietly, "You want the fight stopped, don't you? As soon as that lawman comes to he'll start it again. These Wells Fargo agents don't know how to quit, but if he's trussed up he'll have to."

She looked up at him, uncertain, speculative and after a long moment said, "Then you'd better tie up Wolf too. He was really trying to kill Craig and you mustn't let that happen."

"Wolf's my partner and it would break that up if I put a rope on him. But you're right, he'll be like a bear with a sore paw and a sore head. We'll handle him another way. Here, you hold Lambert's gun on him until I get this one out of trouble in case he wakes up too soon."

He took the weapon out of his belt, put it in her hand and lifted her off the legs, then knelt, knotted the rope around Lambert's ankles, rolled him on his side with his hands behind him, drew the feet up and tied the wrists against the boots and looped the rope around the legs so the man could not pull his feet out of the boots, and stood back.

The girl had walked away and now faced him with Lambert's gun level on Loco, held in both hands with her finger on the trigger. He gave her his warmest smile.

"You going to shoot me, Jerry? What for?"

"I could," she said, her voice anxious. "What do you intend to do about Craig? If you really are wanted I don't believe you would take him to town alive where he could talk to the sheriff, and I am not going to let him be killed."

"That is a puzzle, isn't it? You really love him enough to gun me down? You said a while ago you owed your life to me, and I love you just as much as Lambert."

She chewed her lip but did not lower the gun, saying, "Loco, you are the best friend I ever had and I don't want to hurt you any way. Please don't make me do it."

"Well"—Loco kept smiling—"let's figure out what we can do about this situation."

CHAPTER 18

Wolf Garrison regained consciousness slowly and painfully, his head aching and the sun burning through his eyes. He knew he had been in a fight but he did not know what had knocked him out. It could not have been Lambert. It might have been Loco, but if the positions had been reversed Wolf thought he would have shot both Lambert and Loco, taken Jerry Dillman and ridden out. It surprised him that he was alive.

He opened his eyes and saw Loco squatted beside him, his face thoughtful, and said, "What fell on me, a mountain?"

"Jerry swatted you with a gun a few times."

"She did? Why?"

"You don't remember? You were strangling Lambert. She told you not to. You wouldn't stop so she knocked you out. That little blonde has guts."

"She's a beaut, all right. Help me sit up, and I can use a little water."

Loco gave him a hand, then went for a canteen and Wolf

drank thirstily, regaining his strength rapidly, then looking around to orient where he was. He saw the girl sitting close to Craig Lambert and saw how Lambert was tied and grinned at Loco.

"You truss him that way?"

"Uh-huh."

"Why didn't you blow his head off?"

"Jerry didn't want me to. I tied him so you wouldn't kill him either."

Wolf Garrison thought that over. They had both meant that Lambert should die before they left the Superstitions and now Loco had changed his mind. Garrison wondered at it but by now he knew enough about his partner to respect his judgment.

"I suppose that makes sense. . . ."

"I think so. While you two were out Jerry and I had a pow-wow. She loves that agent so much she was ready to shoot me."

Garrison's head came up sharply. "With what?"

"I gave her Lambert's gun so she'd feel safe enough to listen to reason."

"What kind of reason?"

"I made a deal with her. I tied Lambert up so he couldn't make a break for a sheriff. . . ."

"We'd better cut his throat."

"I told her you'd feel that way. That's why she agreed not to cut him loose until we've had five hours' start."

"You're out of your mind, Loco. I'm not riding out and leaving her here for him. How come you're willing to pass her up?"

"Funny thing about that. This week I found out something. This is one girl I don't want unless she wants me. And she's not for you either."

Wolf got to his feet, saying, "I think different," and walked to Jerry Dillman.

Beside her Craig Lambert lay, his eyes smoking, his voice grating through his teeth. "Garrison, cut me loose and I'll . . ."

Garrison grinned. "What I'll cut is your throat."

The girl's hands were folded in the circle of her crossed legs and she said hurriedly, "Loco promised."

The wolf shrugged. "I'm not bound by what he says. Come here to me."

He reached a hand toward her and hers came out of her lap, bringing Lambert's gun up. Instinctively Wolf slapped at where his holster usually hung. It wasn't there. He backed away slowly.

"Loco, where's my belt?"

Loco was mild. "Hanging on my saddle."

Garrison kept backing until he reached the nearest horse and put his hand behind him, feeling for the boot. He touched the rifle and yanked it out.

Loco said quietly, "It isn't loaded."

For a moment he thought the wolf would rush at him swinging the barrel, then Garrison flung around and rammed the rifle back, growling,

"So let's ride."

"With you in a minute."

Loco Smith took Lambert's belt, walked to the girl and extended his hand for Lambert's gun but she pulled it back.

"It's Craig's. I'm keeping it."

He did not drop the hand. "Not much good empty. I don't want to leave you here half a day with no protection."

Sheepishly she held it toward him and he filled the chambers, dropped the belt and told her, "Five hours, Jerry. If he talks you into starting sooner I'm apt to be behind a cactus and I'll forget how bad you want him."

He handed her the gun again and she stood up to take it. "Shoot," Lambert commanded. "Shoot now."

Instead she stood on tiptoe, put her arms around Loco's neck and kissed him on the mouth. She leaned back, still holding him and said, "Loco Smith, I'm proud to know you. I'll always remember what you've done. Take care of yourself and keep out of trouble."

Loco blushed to the top of his head and ran. In another instant he would forget his noble aberration. He meant to take care of himself, yes, but keeping out of trouble . . . trouble sought him out.

He mounted, waved and turned down canyon at Wolf Garrison's side.

Behind them Craig Lambert fought his rope and pleaded. "Jerry . . . Jerry . . . Don't do this to me. I have to take those men in. They're a danger to the country."

"They're a danger to you if I let you go after them, especially Wolf, and I won't break my promise."

"A promise to outlaws is no promise at all. Jerry, I am a law officer. I can't return the money your father stole but I am duty bound to capture men like those. *Let me go*."

"I will," she said. "In five hours."

"In five hours there can be Apaches swarming over us."

"I'll watch. There's no place close for them to hide and I'll bring your rifle over here."

Lambert groaned. "Jerry, you must not be so stubborn. As a special agent I order you to cut this rope off."

Her blue eyes widened and suddenly she laughed. "As a special agent you are going to have some explaining to do when you marry Dilly Dillman's daughter. You had better resign and find another job."

He looked startled. That thought had not occurred to him, but she was right, married to the highwayman's child he would always be suspect. He could see the shock on Hume's chill face, and that brought his own laughter erupting through his anger.

"I'll make you a deal, Jerry. I'll give you my resignation now and we'll sit here the five hours if you'll let me loose."

"Is a promise to an outlaw's daughter any good?"

"A promise to the woman I'm going to marry is."

She cut away the rope and they waited until the sun was low, then, not daring to stay through the night alone they rode out of the Superstitions.

158

Loco Smith was glad to put those mountains behind him. He had missed finding a fortune, had found and lost a girl, but at least he had a partner at his side, however sulky at the moment. Riding through the pillars that guarded Broken Ax Canyon, Garrison growled,

"When do I get my six-gun and rifle bullets back?"

"As soon as we get to Phoenix."

"What's in Phoenix for us?"

"Maybe nothing, Wolf, but then again . . . That old hatchet face at the hotel wrote Dillman's letter and maybe drew his map. Could be she beat us to the money."

Garrison was scornful of the possibility. "She's not strong enough to move all that sand and rock off, load the money on mules and cover the box up again like we found it."

"If she'd thrown in with Carney he could do the bull work. She might have trusted him, sent him in alone. That lock was opened with a key and she could have got that from Dillman. I want to ask her some questions."

"And I want my hardware. I feel undressed."

"I'll give it to you when you cool off and we're too far from the Superstitions for you to ride back and shoot Lambert and break Jerry's heart. Get your mind off him and think about Mame Carter."

The horses had taken too much in the mountains to do more than walk and they laid over at the bank of the Salt River to rest them and let them graze, so it was midmorning of the third day before they rode into the ragged town and tied up at the hotel rail.

There was no one in the lobby and they went through to the bar. Sam Stovel was leaning against it talking to his brother behind it. Sam turned his head at the sound of the boots, then came full about, astonished.

"You made it back in one piece? What about the blonde and that other fellow?"

"They'll be along," Loco told him.

Sam's eyes were bright with curiosity, his question eager. "You get that fortune Jerry offered me a hunk of?"

Loco said evasively, "It belonged to Wells Fargo. Where can we find the woman who owns the hotel?"

"She doesn't own it any more," Al Stovel said. "I do."

Loco shot a quick glance at Wolf, then looked to Al. "You bought it from her?"

"Nope. Mame said her brother was sick and she had to go take care of him. Walked in here the day after you left and handed me the key, said it was all mine."

"Right generous of her. She say where the brother lives?"

"No, but I put her trunks on the stage for Tucson and they must have been full of lead. Stage driver was back through here day before yesterday, stood right where you are and had a drink and I asked him where Mame went. Funny thing, he said last he saw of her she was getting on a stage for Guaymas down in Mexico, so maybe her brother lives there."

"Maybe." Loco did not sound as if he believed that, nor that the trunks were filled with lead. It went against the grain to have put all the effort into the hunt and lose the treasure to a sly old biddy, but running her down through Mexico could take the rest of his life. He smiled and told Al Stovel, "You tell that to Craig Lambert when he and Jerry come through." The special agent just might be mule-headed enough to go after Mame Carter.

On the street again Wolf Garrison said, "I'm not too comfortable this close to Yuma, Loco, we'd better make a detour if we're going south."

"Go ahead, but I don't think you'll find her this side of the Atlantic."

"You're probably right, so where do we head?"

Loco Smith had a faraway smile, saying, "What about Frisco? They've got a district up there that makes the Superstitions look like the Big Rock Candy Mountains."